"Hello, I'm Ross Peterson."
He held out his hand.

Adrie hesitated a split second, then offered her hand. His grip was firm and confident, his fingers smooth and warm. She looked into his dark brown eyes and dropped his hand. "So, how can I help you?"

"Actually, I think I might be able to help you," Ross said. "I heard you were looking to hire a new manager for the bookstore, and I may be just the man for the job."

Adrie frowned. They needed someone reliable and trustworthy, not a free spirit, adventurous type. The way Ross was dressed, he looked as though he'd just walked off the ferry from a hike up Mount Baker.

Could Ross be the one to step in and take her place, or would he let them down like the last two men they'd hired and then had to fire?

What if she spent weeks training him, then he walked out on them? And there was the obvious problem that he seemed very self-assured and good-looking.

How could you trust a man like that?

Books by Carrie Turansky

Love Inspired

Along Came Love
Seeking His Love
A Man to Trust

CARRIE TURANSKY

and her husband, Scott, live in beautiful central New Jersey. They are blessed with five great kids, a lovely daughter-in-law and an adorable grandson. Carrie homeschools her two youngest children, teaches women's Bible studies and enjoys reading, gardening and walking around the lake near their home. After her family lived in Kenya as missionaries for a year, Carrie missed Africa so much she decided to write a novel set there to relive her experiences. That novel sits on a shelf and will probably never be published, but it stirred her desire to tell stories that touch hearts with God's love. She loves hearing from her readers. You may email her at carrie@carrieturansky.com. You're also invited to visit her website at www.carrieturansky.com.

A Man to Trust
Carrie Turansky

Love Inspired

™ LOVE INSPIRED BOOKS

ISBN-13: 978-0-373-87730-0

A MAN TO TRUST

Copyright © 2012 by Carrie Turansky

www.LoveInspiredBooks.com

Printed in U.S.A.

The Lord is my strength and my shield;
my heart trusts in Him, and He helps me. My heart
leaps for joy, and with my song I praise Him.
—*Psalms* 28:7

To Suzanne, Katy, Claudia and Ellie, my friends and fellow writers, who inspire and encourage me to press on to do my best. Thank you!

Chapter One

Today, of all days, Adrienne Chandler should've been swathed in white chiffon and Belgium lace. Instead, she wore khaki pants and a navy blue knit shirt with the words *Bayside Books* stitched in red over the pocket. Rather than floating down the church aisle on the arm of her father, she hid in the back office of her grandmother's bookstore, hovering over a slightly lopsided birthday cake.

Adrie struck a match and lit the two large purple candles shaped like the numbers seven and zero on top of Nana's cake. With a quick huff, she blew out the match and touched up a spot where the chocolate cake peeked through the pale pink buttercream frosting.

If her life had gone as she'd planned, she'd be enjoying wedding cake rather than birthday cake, but it was time to stop dwelling on what should've been and make today special for her grandma.

Hannah Bodine, curator of Fairhaven's small historical museum and one of her grandma's dearest friends, peeked in the doorway. She held up her bright red cell phone, her cheeks glowing from the warmth of the late summer afternoon. "Your grandmother's on her way!"

Adrie forced a smile. "All right. Let's get the party started."

More than a dozen of her grandmother's friends turned to watch as Adrie walked into the bookstore's café, carrying the cake topped with the blazing purple candles.

"They should be here any second," Hannah announced. "Barb has been keeping Marian busy over at Three French Hens."

Adrie chuckled at the thought of thrifty Nana shopping at the trendy boutique rather than the clearance racks of her favorite department store.

Irene Jameson, another member of her grandma's close-knit group of friends, affectionately known around town as the Bayside Treasures, hurried over. "As soon as they come in, I'll shout surprise, but you start the song, because I sing like an old jaybird."

"Oh, Irene, you don't sound like a jaybird."

"Of course not," Hannah added with a teasing twinkle in her eyes. "She sounds more like an old crow."

Irene gasped, then broke out in giggles and clutched Hannah's arm. "I'll get you for that one."

"Quiet, everyone. They're coming in the front door!" The crowd hushed just as the bell jingled. A few seconds later her grandmother and Barb Gunderson walked toward the back of the store.

"Where's Adrie? I thought she was going to hold down the fort until we got back." Marian Chandler stepped around the end of the bookshelves.

"Surprise! Happy birthday!" The chorus of friends leaped up from the tables, clapping and waving purple balloons and handmade *Happy Birthday* signs.

Adrie walked forward with the glowing cake and started singing.

Nana's expression bloomed from wide-eyed shock to a teary smile. "Thank you all so much. What a wonderful surprise." Her gaze traveled around her circle of friends, then settled on Adrie. "You planned this, didn't you?"

Adrie smiled and shrugged slightly. "Yes, but I had a lot of help from the Bayside Treasures."

"Oh, you darling girl." Nana hugged Adrie, then embraced her fellow Treasures, Hannah, Irene and Barb. "I thought it was odd you had so much trouble making up your mind about that outfit at the boutique," she said to Barb. "Made me wonder if you were losing your grip."

"Not yet, honey." Tall and slim with dark auburn hair, Barb was the youngest of the Bayside Treasures. Though she'd already passed sixty, she still taught more than a dozen piano students each week and played the organ and piano for church services and weddings.

Nana beamed them a bright smile. "So what are we waiting for? Let's eat cake!"

Barb took charge, cutting generous slices. Irene passed them around, while Adrie served coffee and iced tea.

"This is delicious," Pastor James said between bites. "Who baked the cake?"

Irene's cheeks took on a rosy hue, and she ducked her chin.

"Who else?" Hannah slipped her arm around Irene's shoulder. "Everyone knows Irene Jameson is the best baker in Fairhaven."

Adrie smiled and stood back, watching her grandma make the rounds and greet her friends. Her bright blue eyes glowed each time she received a hug or birthday card. Her grandmother had known many of these people for over twenty years, since she and Grandpa Bill had opened Bayside Books. It was the only Christian bookstore in Fairhaven, and it served as a lighthouse to the community and a gathering place for family and friends.

The bell over the front door jingled again, and Adrie glanced down the aisle.

Cameron McKenna, owner of McKenna's Frame Shop, stepped inside. Adrie's friend, Rachel Clark, had recently announced her engagement to Cam, and they were planning an early fall wedding. Adrie released a wistful sigh. At least someone's relationship was working out.

Another man followed Cam through the door. As he came into view, Adrie sucked in a quick breath. For a split second she thought it was her former fiancé, Adam Sheffield, but she quickly realized her mistake. Though his height and coloring were similar, this man's dark brown hair was longer, sweeping across his forehead and touching his collar in the back.

Over his shoulder, he carried what looked like a black leather camera bag. His well-worn jeans and the light blue shirt with the sleeves rolled up sealed the difference. Adam never wore such casual clothes. His were always tailored and professional.

The man's large, dark eyes focused on Adrie. He nodded and sent her a warm smile.

She looked away, trying to shake off her discomfort over his resemblance to Adam.

"Hi, Adrie." Cam crossed toward her. "Looks like there's a party going on."

She looked up at Cam, but her traitorous gaze kept drifting toward the other man. "Yes, we're celebrating Marian's seventieth birthday."

"Sorry, we didn't mean to crash your party," Cam said.

Her eyes snapped back to Cam. "Oh, it's okay. You're welcome to stay. Would you like some cake?"

Cam turned to his friend and lifted one eyebrow.

The man grinned and nodded. "I always say yes to cake."

"Adrie, this is Ross Peterson. Ross, this is Adrienne Chandler. She manages the bookstore with her grandmother."

"Hello, Adrienne." Ross held out his hand.

She hesitated a split second, then offered her hand. His grip was firm and confident, his fingers smooth and warm. She looked into his dark brown eyes, and a ripple of awareness traveled through her. Heat flooded her face. She dropped his hand and turned back to Cam. "So, how can I help you?"

"Actually, I think we might be able to help you," Ross said.

Her gaze darted back to Ross.

"Oh, Cam, Ross, so good to see you!" Hannah bustled over and gave each man a quick hug. She turned and motioned Marian to join them. Hannah knew Cam from the Fairhaven Arts Center. Cam's frame shop was just down the hall from the small historical museum Hannah managed. Cam and Ross greeted Marian and wished her a happy birthday.

"So, did you come for the party, or is there something we can help you with?" Marian asked.

"We heard you were looking to hire a new manager for the bookstore," Cam said.

"That's right. Adrie's been helping me for over a year now, since my husband passed away, but I want to free her up so she can play her flute professionally."

Ross lifted his eyebrows and studied Adrie with renewed interest.

Her face flushed—again.

Cam clamped his hand on his friend's shoulder. "I think Ross might be just the man for the job."

Adrie shot her grandmother a worried glance. They needed someone reliable and trustworthy, not a free spirit, adventurous type. The way Ross was dressed, he looked as though he'd just walked off the ferry from a vacation in the San Juan Islands or a hike up Mount Baker.

"Ross and I have been friends for years," Cam continued.

"And we've also been co-op partners at the Arts Center. I think he could be a big help to you."

Adrie pressed her lips together. Was Cam right? Could Ross be the one to step in and take her place, or would he let them down like the last two men they'd hired and then had to fire—one for stealing and the other for complete incompetence?

He seemed very self-assured and good-looking. How could you trust a man like that?

Nana nodded. "I'm glad you came by. Why don't you have some cake, and as soon as things settle down, we'll talk."

"Thanks." Ross flashed a broad smile, his white teeth contrasting with his tanned face. "I appreciate you meeting with me, especially on your birthday." His smile faded a few watts. "But I'd hate for you to miss your party. Maybe it would be better if I came back tomorrow."

Adrie nodded.

But Marian shook her head. "Oh, it's not a problem, not at all. Come on, let's get some cake for you and Cam."

Adrie closed her eyes. Couldn't her grandma see past his charming smile? How could she be so softhearted and trusting?

A wave of melancholy washed over Adrie. She used to be like that before all the heartbreak she'd faced the last few years, but not anymore. Trust had to be earned, and she hadn't met a man yet who could earn hers.

Ross Peterson was probably no different than the rest. And if that was true, she'd need to be on guard and make sure he didn't take advantage of them.

Thirty minutes later Adrie sat across from Ross and her grandmother while her grandmother conducted the interview with him. The store and café were quiet now. The only other people around were two middle-aged women browsing in the fiction section. Adrie sat facing the sales counter ready to help them if they had questions or wanted to make a purchase.

Nana reviewed Ross's résumé with a warm, pleasant expression on her face. "It looks like you have an excellent education and some good job experience." She looked up. "Tell us about your photography studio."

He frowned slightly, faint lines appearing at the corners of his eyes. "I started out at the Arts Center about three years ago. Things were building slowly over the first two years, but it's been tough this last year with the bad economy. I didn't want to go into debt, so I closed up shop a couple months ago."

"We've had a slump over the last year, as well," Nana said. "But fall tends to be our busiest season, so we're hoping things will improve." She checked the second page of his résumé. "You've invested quite a few years in photography. You're not planning to give that up altogether, are you?"

"No, I'd like to do it on the side."

Adrie studied him, trying to figure out the man behind the handsome exterior. What were his real motives for wanting this job? And how did he expect to continue his photography work while he managed the bookstore? This was a full-time job that would become more demanding as they moved into the holiday season.

"I believe you have the skills for the business side of things," Nana said. "But working here would be quite different than running a photo studio."

"In what way?"

"I consider this store a ministry as well as a business. Many of our customers come in with questions and problems. Some are hurting and need compassion and direction."

He nodded, his expression thoughtful, but Adrie couldn't tell what he really thought of her grandma's comment.

"I'm looking for a manager who can connect with people,

someone who is willing to listen and can offer encouragement and prayer. Would you be comfortable with that?"

He rubbed his chin. "My faith is important to me, but I'm a relatively new believer." He glanced toward the bookshelves. "I've always loved to read, so walking in here and seeing all the titles makes me feel a little like a kid in a candy store." He grinned at her grandmother, his dark eyes taking on a mischievous light.

Adrie rolled her eyes. It was time to cut to the chase and see where he really stood. "I'd like to ask Ross a few questions."

Her grandma looked her way. "Okay, dear, go ahead."

"Could you tell us where you attend church?"

Ross stared at her for a second. "I've gone to Grace Chapel a few times with Cam and Rachel."

She'd never seen him there. But with two services and over five hundred people attending, it was possible she could've missed him.

"We attend Grace Chapel, as well," Nana added, sending Adrie a questioning glance.

"Don't you find it hard to grow spiritually if you aren't committed to a church?" Adrie asked.

He shifted in his chair, looking uncomfortable. "I think being involved in a church is a good thing, but there are other ways a person can grow spiritually."

She tried to keep a neutral expression. "What would you recommend?"

He glanced toward the window. "Spending time in nature helps me connect with God." He looked around the store. "And of course reading spiritual books can help, too."

That was enough for Adrie to make up her mind. "Well, Ross, we appreciate you coming in," she said, ignoring her grandma's wide-eyed look of censure, "but we need someone who's knowledgeable about their faith and can help our customers choose the right resources. So I don't think—"

Nana squeezed Adrie's hand under the table. "I'd like to hear a bit more from Ross. Then I'd like to pray about it before I make a decision."

Adrie stared at her grandma. Was she serious? Why would she even consider hiring someone who obviously wasn't right for the job?

Nana's steady gaze rested on Adrie, her intention clear.

Her grandmother owned the store and would make the final decision. But why would she promise to pray about it? Hiring Ross Peterson would obviously be a mistake.

Ross climbed into the passenger seat of Cam's forest-green SUV and pulled the door closed with more force than needed. But it didn't relieve his frustration. He grabbed his sunglasses from his shirt pocket and slid them into place while his stomach churned.

"So, how did it go?" Cam started the engine, checked over his shoulder and pulled into the street.

"Not too well." Ross clamped his jaw and looked out the side window.

"How come? I thought you'd be perfect for the job."

"I am, but that doesn't seem to matter." He shook his head. What was he going to do now? Since he'd closed his studio, his photography business had dwindled, and he'd had to dip into his savings. Rent on his apartment was due in two weeks along with his car insurance and a few other bills. That would wipe out his reserves.

"That had to be the toughest interview I've ever had."

"I'm surprised. Marian Chandler is one of the sweetest ladies in town."

"She might be, but that granddaughter of hers is another story." Acid burned his throat as he thought of how Adrie had studied him throughout the interview. Each time he answered a question, he could see the doubt in her expression.

Cam grinned. "I thought she seemed a little cool toward you."

"Cool? It was more like freezing."

Cam's grin faded. "I wonder what's up with that."

"I have no idea. She seemed to have her mind set against me before the interview even started." He rubbed his chin, trying to figure out what he'd done to invoke such animosity in her. "What do you know about her?"

"Only what Rachel has told me. Her parents are missionaries in Africa. She was raised there, then she came back to Fairhaven to live with her grandparents and attend college."

"Wow, Africa. That's different."

"Yeah. I think it was Kenya. She must have some great stories, but she never says much about it. The few times we've talked, it's always been about church, work or friends." He tapped his finger on the steering wheel. "She plays the flute with the worship team. Have you seen her at church?"

Ross shook his head. He had only started attending Grace Chapel the last couple of months, after the bottom fell out of his business and Cam had talked to him about the importance of trusting God with his life and future.

He didn't think he'd ever seen Adrie there. He would've remembered her. As a photographer, he always noticed people with unique features and hair color, and Adrie had both. Her dark auburn hair had golden highlights. It curled around her face, then flowed down over her shoulders in soft waves. A fringe of dark lashes framed her large, lavender-blue eyes. Her skin was light and almost translucent like a piece of fine china. Her lips…

He stopped there. What was the point? Beautiful or not, she acted as cold as a glacier toward him. And she seemed intent on convincing her grandmother not to hire him.

"Hey, Ross. Are you off in dreamland?"

He glanced at Cam. "Sorry. What did you say?"

"I asked if you think there's a chance you'll get the job."

He grimaced and shook his head. "No way, not in a million years."

Adrie took another sip of hot orange spice tea, hoping the warmth would soothe the uneasy feelings swirling through her. These Sunday morning breakfasts with her grandma were usually one of her favorite times of the week, but today's conversation was twisting her stomach into a nervous knot.

"I'm sorry, Adrie. I know you're not in favor of hiring Ross, but you haven't given me one solid reason not to."

Adrie set her teacup back on the table. "I know he seems to have good qualifications, but there's something about him that makes me uncomfortable. I'm sorry, Nana, but I don't think we should trust him."

"Those are just feelings, dear, not facts."

"But doesn't God work through our feelings? Aren't we supposed to have peace about our decisions?"

Marian released a soft sigh. "I believe God gives us discernment and wisdom to make decisions when we ask Him for His help. Our feelings play a part in that, but we also need to look at the facts. In this case, Ross has the experience needed, and he has a young, growing faith. Cam seems to know him quite well, and that gives him a solid character reference."

Adrie took another bite of Nana's chocolate-chip coffee cake, giving her time to think before she answered. "But we need a manager who's caring, someone who'll give our customers solid advice. I don't think he has the knowledge or spiritual maturity to do that."

"But he's eager to learn. I could see that in his eyes."

Adrie clicked her tongue. "Please don't get taken in by those delicious dark eyes of his."

Nana's hand stilled as she reached for her coffee cup. A

slow smile spread across her lips. "Did you say his eyes were delicious?"

Adrie's cheeks flamed. "What I meant was, good looks have nothing to do with character. Men who are good-looking tend to know it and use it to their advantage."

Sadness softened Nana's expression. "Oh, honey, not every man you meet is going to treat you like that dreadful Adam Sheffield."

Adrie's heart twisted. "I know. I'm not saying he would."

Painful memories swirled through her mind, taunting her. She would be leaving for her honeymoon today if Adam hadn't walked away and broken every promise he had ever made. She forced those painful thoughts back into the secret corner of her heart and locked them away.

They had nothing to do with Ross Peterson. But was she letting his resemblance to Adam color her judgment? She *had* mistaken him for Adam at first glance.

No. That wasn't it. She was just being cautious, looking out for her grandmother and considering what was best for the business.

Adrie looked across the table at her grandmother. "Promise me you'll think about this a little longer before you make a decision."

Nana patted her hand, her gaze tender. "All right, dear. I'll pray about it some more. But Ross deserves an answer as soon as I can give it."

Looking into her grandma's eyes, she had a dreadful feeling the decision was already made.

Chapter Two

Sunlight sparkled across the rippling surface of Bellingham Bay, blinking back at Ross as he jogged along the South Bay Trail. Snow-white seagulls with gray wingtips and tails swooped overhead, riding the salty breeze. A bird's cry cut through the morning stillness, along with the rhythmic thump of his running shoes hitting the wooden boardwalk. If he could just keep running, maybe he could escape all the discouraging thoughts that weighed him down.

Time to get a grip and think about something positive. He might not have his photography studio anymore, but he still had a few jobs lined up, including Cam and Rachel's wedding next month. If that went well, he might get some referrals for other events. Over time, he could rebuild his business.

Reality rushed back, taking his spirits for a nosedive. Shooting one wedding was not going to turn everything around. He needed a full-time job soon, or his bank account was going to bottom out.

His cell phone buzzed, and he lifted it from his pocket. His father's name and Tacoma number lit up the screen. He shot off a quick prayer for help. Preparing for battle, he tapped the screen and lifted the phone to his ear. "Hey, Dad. How are you doing?"

"If you really wanted to know, you would've answered the last two times I called."

Ross grimaced and slowed to a walk. "Sorry, Dad."

"What, no excuses? No comeback? That's not like you."

Ross swallowed the sharp reply rising in his throat. He had been praying about his strained relationship with his parents. Maybe this call was an answer to those prayers. But if that was true, why did it feel more like a dreaded exam?

"So what's going on? Why haven't we heard from you? Your mother is worried."

Ross paced over to the railing and breathed out slowly, letting go of his desire to be understood by his father. "You're right, Dad. I should've called."

Silence buzzed along the phone line for a few seconds, then his dad cleared his throat. "So, how's the job hunt going? Any leads?"

Ross gazed across the bay toward the hazy blue San Juan Islands. "I had an interview yesterday." He didn't think he'd get the job at the bookstore, but at least it gave him something he could report to his father.

"So, what's the position? Not one of those dead-end photo studio jobs, I hope."

Ross gripped the rough wooden railing. "It's a management position at a bookstore."

"Retail?" His father huffed, his voice heavy with disdain. "Come on, Ross. You can do better than that."

The comment gouged old wounds. "You don't even know anything about the job."

"It's retail!" his father barked as though that was reason enough. "You'd be living paycheck to paycheck."

Ross clamped his jaw, determined not to admit he hadn't even discussed the salary with Marian Chandler.

"I paid a lot of money to put you through college. You shouldn't be wasting your time selling books."

"It's not a waste of time to run a store that offers the community products they need." No way would he tell his father it was a Christian bookstore. That would really set him off.

His father made a harsh noise in his throat. "How would this bookstore business be any better than that photography studio? You gave that a try, and it didn't work."

"It's the economy, Dad. It's been rough for everyone. You can't blame me for that."

"No, but it proves what I've been telling you for years. You need a more dependable career. Not some fly-by-night artistic thing." His father didn't have a creative bone in his body. He had been a CPA for thirty-five years, and he'd never understood how his son could be so different.

"Thanks, Dad." Ross couldn't keep the sarcasm out of his voice.

It didn't seem to faze his father. "Look, son, it's time to come back home to Tacoma and work for me, like we planned."

Ross's stomach clenched. "You mean, like *you* planned."

His father huffed.

"I'm sorry, Dad. I'm not the CPA type. I never will be."

"You'll do what you need to do to support yourself and your family."

"I don't have a family, and it's a good thing because I couldn't live like that."

"But you have no problem with working retail at a bookstore?"

"It sounds interesting to me. And just because I closed the studio, that doesn't mean I'm giving up photography. I have some jobs lined up for weekends and evenings. In a few months, maybe a year, I'm going to open my studio again."

"Now you're dreaming."

Fire infused Ross's face. "Why can't you support me, just a little?"

"I have supported you, all the way through college. Then I helped you set up that studio. And look what happened."

Ross closed his eyes as years of hurtful words and cutting remarks rushed over him like the rising tide. *Lord, help me! If I don't hang up now I'm going to say something I'll regret.* "Dad, I've got to go."

"All right. But you need to call your mother tomorrow. It's her birthday. You know how upset she'll be if she doesn't hear from you."

Ross swallowed hard. "I'll call. I promise."

Adrie knelt and checked the books on the bottom shelf in the biography section. She turned face out a stack of an inspiring missionary's life story. It was one of her favorites, and she always kept several copies on hand so she could recommend it to anyone who was considering serving overseas or going into some type of ministry.

Her hand stilled. Who would recommend it after she left? Ross Peterson certainly didn't know anything about it or any of the other important books in the store.

Who would help the young woman recovering from an abusive childhood find the right book—one that would give her the hope and freedom she needed? What about the grieving man who had lost his wife and needed to know the truth about heaven? Or the frustrated mom or dad searching for practical parenting solutions? So much wisdom and comfort was available on these shelves, but most of their customers needed guidance to find the right resource.

Her shoulders sagged, and her gaze shifted to her grandmother's closed office door. Why was her meeting with Ross taking so long? Was he trying to negotiate a higher salary or a lighter schedule so he could fit in his photography jobs?

Her grandmother was offering a good salary, and she was willing to continue working part-time to give him a flexible schedule. He had probably already accepted the job, and they were just working out the details.

The bell jingled over the front door, and their hefty, fifty-something mailman, Les Hawkins, ambled in, followed by her grandma's friends Barb, Irene and Hannah. It must be almost three o'clock, time for the Bayside Treasures to gather in the café for their weekly Scrabble game and gab session.

"Afternoon, Adrie." Les shuffled over as he pulled a stack of mail from his brown leather bag. She greeted him and accepted the circulars and envelopes.

"It sure is hot out there." He shifted the shoulder strap of his bag, pulled a red bandanna from his back pocket and wiped his glistening forehead. "Can you whip me up one of those strawberry-banana smoothies?"

"I'll get that for you." Barb smiled at Les as she passed and headed toward the café counter.

"Thanks, Barb," Adrie called, holding back a chuckle. Barb had a soft spot in her heart for Les, though he seemed clueless.

"How are you doing, honey?" Irene asked and gave her a quick one-arm hug. "You look so pretty, today. I love that lavender color on you. And with your hair and eyes—wow!"

Adrie kissed Irene's cheek. "Thanks. You always say the sweetest things."

"Well, it's true. You look beautiful." Irene's smile was contagious, and Adrie couldn't help feeling loved whenever Irene was around. She seemed to have that effect on everyone.

Irene set a large plastic container on the table containing her famous cookies. Irene made a new batch every Monday to supply the café regulars. Adrie's mouth watered just thinking about the delicious chocolate cookies. They tasted like the best brownies you could imagine, but were chewy and crispy around the edges.

"Look what my son gave me." Hannah held out a new Scrabble game.

Adrie grinned. "What's wrong with the other one?"

"We just about wore out that old board."

"Some of the tiles were missing, too," Barb added, then hit the button on the blender. The whirring sound filled the air for a few seconds. Barb poured the smoothie into a tall plastic cup. "Here you go, Les. Hope you like it."

"Thanks. This will hit the spot." He slurped a big gulp. "Delicious!" Then he tipped his hat and headed for the door. "You ladies have a nice day now."

"Bye, Les. See you tomorrow," Adrie called.

"Where's Marian?" Hannah asked, pulling the cellophane off the new Scrabble box. "It's already ten past three."

Adrie pointed toward her grandma's office. "She's meeting with Ross Peterson." Just saying his name made her stomach tighten. She tried to push her negative feelings aside. The decision was made. She had to accept it and make the best of the situation.

Irene looked up. "Oh, you mean that handsome young man we met at Marian's party?"

Hannah nodded. "Marian's hiring him for the manager's position." She turned to Adrie. "I think you'll really like working with him. He's got a great way with people—and best of all—he's single." Her eyes glowed and she lifted her silver eyebrows.

Adrie quickly looked away and bit her tongue. Would these ladies ever give up?

Irene smiled, her eyes wide and encouraging. "Maybe you can start auditioning for orchestras now."

"Yes, we don't want all your musical talent and training to go to waste," Barb added.

Hannah tossed the cellophane in the trash. "It's not wasted. Adrie plays at church almost every week."

"I know, but she's been wanting to play professionally for years. And if Ross helps Marian manage the store, Adrie will be free to move away and play her flute like she always wanted." Barb turned to Adrie. "Won't that be wonderful?"

Adrie tried to answer, but unexpected tightness clogged her throat. "Yes. That'll be great," she finally managed to say.

What was the matter with her? Of course she wanted to audition and eventually play her flute full-time. She'd been working toward that for fourteen years—all the lessons and hours of practice, all those summers at Morrowstone Music Festival, first as a student and then being accepted for a fellowship. It looked like she'd finally have the freedom to strike out on her own, leave Fairhaven behind and follow her dream.

But was she ready to leave her grandmother and their bookstore under Ross Peterson's care?

The sound of Scrabble tiles spilling on the table brought her back to the moment.

"So, how was your date last night?" Hannah asked Adrie as she poured the tiles into the black cloth bag.

"Oh, yes, tell us all about it." Irene smiled expectantly and settled in the chair across from Hannah. "Noah seems like such a nice young man."

Adrie held back a grimace. Ever since Adam broke their engagement, her grandmother and her friends seemed determined to help her find a new Mr. Right. She'd put them off for months, refusing to let them introduce her to anyone. Finally, last week, she had agreed to a blind date with Irene's nephew's roommate, Noah, hoping that would satisfy them and they'd stop hounding her.

No such luck.

"So what do you think? Is Noah a keeper?" Hannah looked up, a hopeful gleam in her soft brown eyes.

"Wait," Barb called from behind the café counter. "Don't say a word until I get there." She hustled over, wiping her hands on a towel. "Okay. Give us details. How was the date?"

Adrie laughed. What else could she do? "Noah and I didn't exactly hit it off."

Irene's ever-present smile faded. "Really? Why not?"

"Anyone who announces he was a Persian prince in his former life, and then uses eyedrops, nose drops and cough drops all within one hour…just isn't my kind of guy."

Hannah gasped. "You're kidding! He did all that?"

Adrie nodded. "And he spent the rest of the evening talking about his food allergies and the cockroach invasion of his apartment."

"Oh my." Irene lifted her hand to cover her mouth, then dissolved into giggles. Barb and Hannah joined in, snickering and laughing until tears rolled down their cheeks.

Sure, it was funny now. But last night was an awful experience Adrie did not want to repeat. She had to put an end to their matchmaking schemes.

"All right, listen up!" She jammed her hands on her hips. "This is it. No more dates—blind or otherwise! Don't even try to set me up with anyone. I won't go!" The women continued to chuckle and grin at her. "I mean it! I've sworn off men altogether!"

Irene's gaze traveled past Adrie's shoulder, and her giggles faded. Barb shot Adrie a warning glance, while Hannah coughed to smother her laughter.

A sinking feeling hit Adrie's stomach. Slowly, she turned and looked over her shoulder. Ross Peterson and Nana stood behind her. She cringed and her face flamed. How much of her anti-dating tirade had Ross heard?

* * *

Ross did his best to hold back a grin, but his lips twitched with the effort. Adrie's declaration against dating had been delivered with so much gusto he couldn't help it. Too bad he hadn't heard the story that prompted it, because it must've been a good one.

Her cheeks flushed a pretty hot pink. She seemed to melt a little as she rubbed her forehead, shielding her eyes from him.

Marian cleared her throat and placed her hand on Ross's shoulder. "Well, ladies, I'd like you to meet the new manager-in-training of Bayside Books."

"Congratulations!" Irene gave him a hug. Hannah patted him on the shoulder, and Barb nodded her approval. But Adrie leaned back against the counter and studied him through cloudy, gray-blue eyes.

"Oh, this is going to be wonderful." Irene beamed at Marian. "Now you can cut back your hours and have fun with us, and Adrie can spend more time on her music."

Marian nodded. "I'm sure with Ross here, we're all going to be very happy."

His gaze traveled around the group of women, then settled on Adrie. Her apprehensive expression made him doubt she agreed with her grandmother on that point.

Marian snapped her fingers. "Oh, I forgot the keys. I'll be right back." She headed to the office.

Marian's offer of free rent on one of the apartments above the bookstore was an unexpected perk. Of course he hadn't seen it yet, but her description made it sound better than his current place. And living upstairs would certainly make it an easy commute.

A few seconds later, Marian returned with the keys. "Let's go upstairs, and you can take a look."

Adrie's eyes widened, and the color drained from her face. "You're showing him the apartment?"

Marian turned around. "Yes. Won't it be great to have him right here in the building, especially if there are any emergencies? I haven't been happy about you being up there all by yourself."

Ross's steps slowed. Adrie lived upstairs? Marian had failed to mention there were two apartments above the store. Well, he supposed being neighbors wouldn't be too bad. It might even give him an opportunity to convince her he wasn't the enemy.

Chapter Three

Ross shoved the cardboard box across the bare hardwood floor of his new apartment and added it to the growing pile in the corner of his bedroom. Stashing all his photography studio equipment here felt like swallowing a bitter pill, but he couldn't afford to pay for a storage unit. Unfortunately, that meant he'd see it each morning when he woke up and every evening when he went to bed—a stark reminder his business had failed.

His father's words ran through his mind again. *You need a dependable career, not some fly-by-night artistic thing. I paid a lot of money to put you through college. You shouldn't be wasting your time selling books.*

He sighed heavily, and rubbed the back of his neck. When would he be able to set up his studio again? Six months? A year? Or would his dream die while he spent most of his time working at the bookstore just so he could pay his bills?

Why is this happening, God? I thought getting to know You meant my life was going to get easier, not harder. Shaking his head, he pushed those questions away.

This was not time for stinkin' thinkin', as his friend Cam would say. Negative thoughts and self-doubt would just pull him down. He had to hang on to the truth or he would sink under all these difficulties. Closing his eyes, he breathed in deeply and focused his thoughts. God was in control. He had a plan. His responsibility was to pray, listen for God's direction, and trust Him for the future.

Things would get better. The economy would pick up. He would get back on his feet. His time at the bookstore would not be wasted. As long as he stayed connected to God and paid attention to where He was leading, he would be okay.

Give me the courage to believe that. Help me trust You. Slowly, a sense of peace eased away the strain of the day. It gave him a new surge of energy to get moving again.

Returning to the living room, he surveyed the six large cartons by the front door. Several more were piled on the couch and chairs. A heap of shirts and pants, still on their hangers, lay draped over the coffee table. Bags of groceries and boxes of kitchen items sat on the floor in the small kitchen. What a mess. He hoped to sort things out this afternoon, because tomorrow morning at nine he started working at the bookstore.

He left to bring in the last load from the car. As he passed Adrienne's apartment, flute music floated into the hall.

His steps slowed. How often did she play? Would she keep him up at night with her practice sessions? His flash of irritation faded as he listened to the series of notes that rose and fell like water pouring from a fountain. He leaned closer, waiting. After a short pause, she started again, repeating the same notes with more strength. Even though the door separated them, he could feel the emotion in her music.

She was good, very good. He stared at the door, waiting for the next part of the haunting melody to reach his ears. Suddenly, he stopped and looked around. What if she caught him lurking by her door, eavesdropping? That would certainly seal her negative opinion of him. He shook his head and hustled down the hall, then took the steps two at a time.

With a mocking laugh at himself, he pushed open the door leading to the back parking lot.

Lifting his gaze to Adrienne's window, he listened, but he couldn't hear her flute anymore, and he missed the music.

Adrie lifted the flute to her lips and pulled in a deep breath. Focusing on the key signature, she ticked off the beat and launched into Bach's Partita. With her eyes closed, she let the notes ebb and flow, the music pouring from her soul.

A crash in the hallway startled her. *What in the world?* Lowering her flute, she hurried to the door and pulled it open.

Ross Peterson lay sprawled on the hall floor, hundreds of old-fashioned photography slides scattered around him like piles of leaves on a late fall day.

She leaned out the door. "Are you okay?"

He looked up, his dark eyes wide. "Yeah. I'm fine."

"What happened?"

He rose to his knees. "I tripped."

She wasn't thrilled about having him as a neighbor, but she couldn't very well close the door and let him clean up the mess by himself. With a resigned sigh, she carefully laid aside her flute and joined him on the hallway floor.

"You've got quite a collection here."

"Yep." He scooped up a stack of slides and shoved them in a small cardboard box.

"You don't see many of these anymore."

"Nope." His face looked flushed as he focused on filling the box rather than looking at her.

His embarrassment was sort of cute. She suppressed a smile as she lifted up a slide to the hall light, but she couldn't see the image clearly. "So is this how you keep all your photos?"

"Oh, these aren't mine. They're my grandfather's."

"He's a photographer, too?"

"He had a studio in Tacoma for over forty years. He even had some of his photos published." Ross stopped for a moment. "When I was twelve, he gave me my first camera and taught me how to use it. I probably never would've gotten into photography if it wasn't for him." Warmth filled his voice, and his embarrassment seemed to fade.

"Sounds like you two are pretty close."

"We were." His smile faded. "He passed away last April."

She bit her lip. "I'm sorry. My grandpa died not too long ago. I can relate."

"Marian's husband?"

"Yes. He passed away a year ago last May."

"Marian mentioned him a couple times today."

She nodded. "They were very close. I know she still misses him. Me, too."

Ross cocked his head. "What was he like?"

She sat back on her heels. "He loved playing backgammon, watching baseball and going fishing. He loved to read, too. He and my grandma were married for forty-eight years. They started the bookstore together when I was just a baby."

"So you grew up hanging around here?"

"Only for the first few years, then our family...moved away." She didn't often tell people she'd spent most of her life in Kenya. It required too much explanation and usually left her feeling like an oddball. But for some reason she wanted to see Ross's reaction to that news. "Actually, I grew up in Kenya. My parents are still missionaries there."

He nodded, as though that wasn't unusual at all. "Sounds interesting."

Was he just making conversation or was he truly interested? She couldn't tell, so she kept quiet and picked up a few more slides.

He watched her, his gaze steady. "That must have been quite an adventure growing up in Africa. I'd like to hear more about it sometime."

She ducked her head and smiled. "Most people fade out as soon as I say the words *missionaries* or *Kenya*."

"Not me. I've always dreamed of going to Africa. When I was a kid I read every copy of my grandpa's *National Geographic* cover to cover." He grinned, his dark eyes glowing. "I'd love to go on a safari someday. Maybe track down some lions and cheetahs or follow a herd of elephants." His enthusiasm for the place she loved stirred her heart.

"If you ever do plan a trip, let me know. I could tell you about the different game parks and give you some suggestions."

He nodded, his smile warm and confident. "Thanks. That would be great. It's just a dream right now, but I'll make it there someday."

She couldn't help returning his smile. "I think you will."

Ross shot a longing look toward the bookstore's café area as he and Adrie walked past. Maybe a second cup of coffee would help him remember all the details she was giving him as they toured the bookstore. His mouth watered as they passed the glass display case of tempting bakery treats. One of those apple walnut muffins would really hit the spot.

"This is the Christian living section," Adrie said, drawing his attention back to the bookshelves. "Here you have books about the Holy Spirit, discipleship, charismatic interest and general topics." She lifted her eyebrows, silently asking him if he had any questions.

He wasn't exactly sure what charismatic interests might be, but if he asked her now, that would extend the tour and delay his coffee break. He'd figure it out later.

She motioned toward the next shelf. "This is our prayer, devotional and gift book section."

"Okay." At least he knew what that meant.

"And over here we have the Bible studies and reference

tools, like commentaries, concordances and Bible dictionaries."

He scanned the titles and pulled a large, heavy book off the shelf. "Wow, Strong's Concordance." He chuckled and raised it like he was pumping weights. "Just toting this around would make you *strong* even if you never cracked open the cover." Grinning, he waited for her reaction, but her serious expression didn't change. He sighed and replaced the book.

Ever since they'd started working together this morning, he'd been trying to get her to smile or at least relax a little, but none of his usual methods seemed to work.

"This is our fiction section," she continued. "We have a wide range of novels for men, women and teens—everything from suspense and legal thrillers to gentle Amish stories, along with a lot of historical, women's fiction and romance."

"Ah, now there's a topic I need to read up on." He winked and sent her a teasing grin.

Her cheeks flushed, and she led him around the corner, bringing them closer to the café again. The scent of something freshly baked floated past.

He rubbed his rumbling stomach. "Would you mind if we took a break for a few minutes?"

She frowned slightly and checked her watch. "All right, but we open in ten minutes."

"This won't take long." He rounded the café counter. "Would you like some coffee?"

"I don't drink coffee." She followed him into the café prep area.

He lifted his eyes to the ceiling and sighed. He should've known. "What do you drink?"

"I prefer tea." Her voice carried a hint of a challenge.

"I can make tea."

"I don't think so. Not for me."

Why did she have to be so difficult? Couldn't she just try

to get along? He turned to face her. "What's so hard about pouring hot water in a cup and adding a tea bag? I may be a newbie at the bookstore business, but I think I know how to make a cup of tea." He took a deep breath, trying to calm his thundering pulse. Why was he getting so upset?

A slight smile tipped up one corner of her mouth. "I'm sure you do, just not the way I like it."

Determined not to let her get the best of him, he said, "Well, then why don't you teach me?" He pointed toward the bookshelves. "You have to train me in every other facet of bookstore management, you might as well show me how to make the perfect cup of tea."

A dimple appeared in her left cheek as she smiled. "Okay. If you really want to know, I'll show you how I learned to make tea in Kenya."

"Fine." He crossed his arms and studied her as she took a pan from the cabinet and set it on the small stovetop. His irritation dissolved as he watched her fluid, graceful movements. The overhead lights made her long wavy hair glow with golden threads of fire. He frowned and glanced away. Appreciating her beauty was one thing, staring at her for an extended time was only going to get him into more trouble.

"First thing you need to know is that we call it *chai*."

He'd heard of chai, but he thought it was Indian not African.

"You pour in a cup of milk, and then add a cup of water. Next you add two teaspoons of tea leaves." From a small metal tin, she scooped out two spoonfuls, and dumped them right into the pan.

"Yikes! You drink the leaves?" He leaned forward to take a look.

She laughed softly. "No, you strain them out. But you're getting ahead of me." She popped the lid off the sugar container. "Next you add some sugar." She poured two heaping spoonfuls into the pan and stirred. "Now you let it simmer for a few minutes."

He stepped closer and looked over her shoulder as she swirled the tea leaves in the milky liquid. The steam from the tea rose, bringing with it a distinctive scent, but another fragrance teased his nose. He quietly sniffed and realized the light flowery fragrance must be coming from Adrie's hair.

"So what do you think?" She glanced over her shoulder at him, her eyes like shimmering pools of lavender light.

He swallowed and broke his gaze. "It looks…interesting."

"That seems to be one of your favorite words."

"What?"

"*Interesting.* You use it all the time."

He felt his face heating up. "Okay. I'll make a note of it."

She chuckled as she took two mugs from the shelf over the sink.

"What's so funny?"

"You are." She smiled at him, her eyes dancing with amusement.

Now his face felt like it was on fire. This girl was maddening. Totally maddening! The only time she would smile or laugh was when he felt so embarrassed and frustrated he was ready to pop a cork.

She strained the chai into two mugs and held one out to him. "Here you go."

He was a coffee man—a committed connoisseur of cappuccinos, lattes and espressos. But there was no way he could refuse when she offered him tea with that inviting smile. "Thanks." He accepted the mug and took a sip. The warm, creamy drink flooded his mouth with a sweet tangy flavor.

"So, what do you think? Do you like it?"

He lifted his mug in a toast to her. "This is definitely the best chai I've ever had."

She sent him a delighted look. "Really?"

"Yes…of course it's the only chai I've ever had, but—"

"Oh! You're awful!" She gave him a playful shove.

"No, I'm not." He grinned. "Just a truthful guy who loves to tease a little. But I'm totally enjoying my first cup of chai."

Her smile returned, and a new light sparkled in her eyes.

His spirits soared. He'd finally made a connection with her.

"Time to open up," Marian called, jingling her keys as she walked past, headed toward the front door. "Something tells me it's going to be a great day."

Ross winked at Adrie over the rim of his mug and took another sip of chai. "I believe it is."

Ten minutes later Ross stood by Adrie as she pulled a box cutter from her skirt pocket and slit open a carton of books. He reached down and folded back the flaps for her, revealing the stacks of new books. "How do you know where to put them?"

"Just check the info on the back." She pulled out a book, flipped it over, and pointed to the lower right-hand corner. "It tells you what type of book it is right here."

Ross nodded, reaching into the box to lift out a few more copies. This didn't look hard. She'd given him the tour, and there were signs on the shelves denoting the different sections.

The phone rang, and Adrie looked up. "I need to get that. I'll be right back. Do what you can." She sent him a doubtful glance, then crossed the store and slipped behind the sales counter.

He turned over the first book. *Christian Living/Personal Growth/Women/Discipleship.* Frowning, he scratched his chin. They had both a Christian living section and a women's section. Where was he supposed to put this title?

The bell over the door jingled. He looked around for

Marian, but he didn't see her. Adrie was still behind the counter, holding the phone between her shoulder and ear while she made notes on a pad. Guess it was up to him to greet their first customer of the day.

A middle-aged woman with short gray hair stepped in and looked around with a nervous glance.

He straightened and offered her a smile. "Good morning. Can I help you find something?"

"I just want to look around." Her clothes—worn jeans and faded red T-shirt with the words *The Chuckanut Radio Hour* printed on the front—suggested she was a local, though she didn't seem to be familiar with the store.

"Take your time. If you need any help, just let me know." He picked up a book from the box and read the back cover information.

"Could I take a look at that?" The woman pointed to the title he held in his hand.

"Sure." He passed her the book, *Hope in Hard Times*.

Tears glistened in her eyes as she focused on the beautiful seascape on the cover. "I'm going through a hard time right now, and I'm fresh out of hope, that's for sure."

Anguished questions filled the woman's eyes. "Is this a good author?"

He swallowed hard. "Mrs. Chandler and her granddaughter, Adrienne, select all the books for the store. I'm sure they only bring in authors they trust."

Biting her lower lip, the woman turned over the book and read the back.

Had he given her the right direction? He shoved his hands in his pants pockets and silently breathed out a prayer. *Lord, this woman needs more help than I can give her. Would You give me a hand?*

She looked up, blinking back tears in her tired brown eyes. "I lost my job yesterday."

Her words hit him like a punch in the stomach. "I'm

sorry." It wasn't hard for him to recall how miserable it felt to be without a job, uncertain how you'd pay the rent or buy groceries.

"My husband has been out of work for over a year, since the cannery closed. I'm not sure what we're going to do now. He's diabetic, and we lost our insurance." She shook her head, weary lines of defeat creasing her forehead.

"Why don't you sit down and take a look at this book?" He guided her to an overstuffed chair in the corner. "I'll check around and see what else I can find for you."

He shot off another quick prayer as he scanned the shelves. He snagged two other titles that looked encouraging.

She looked up as he approached. "Is it okay if I just sit here for a few minutes and read several pages? I need to be sure about the book before I spend any money."

"Sure. Take your time. Here are a couple more you might like." He set them on the small table beside her, then glanced down the aisle at the box of books waiting to be shelved. Giving her some books to browse didn't seem like it was enough.

Memories of his talks with Cam over the last few months rose in his mind. Those conversations had given him the courage and hope he needed while he was jobless and wondering how he would make it until a new job came through. Maybe he could help this woman the same way Cam had helped him.

He pushed away his discomfort and squatted down next to her chair. "I'm sorry you're going through a rough time. I know what it's like to be out of work. I lost my job a few months ago."

Her eyebrows rose. "You did?"

He nodded. "This is actually my first day working at this new job."

A slight smile tipped up one side of her mouth. "Your first

day. Wow. It must feel good knowing you'll have a paycheck coming in soon."

"Yes, I'm thankful." He glanced around the store. "It's a whole new line of work for me, but I think I'm going to like it." He turned back to her. "And what about you? What kind of job are you looking for?"

"I'm a dog groomer," she said with a bashful smile. "I've been doing that for about ten years, but the shop where I've been working just closed. The owner decided to retire."

He nodded and settled on the floor beside her chair ready to listen as she told him the rest of her story.

Adrie hung up the phone and made a final note about the inventory system Chuck at Village Books had recommended. Faint sounds of conversation at the other end of the store registered in her mind. She looked up and cocked her head to listen, but the words were unclear. Suddenly, her pulse jumped. Ross must be talking to a customer. She tossed aside her pen and hustled around the counter and down the aisle. Her steps stalled when she reached the end.

Ross knelt next to a plump woman in her fifties. She was seated in the blue overstuffed chair by the front window. Both their heads were bowed, and his hand rested lightly on her shoulder. Tears slipped down the woman's weathered cheeks as she held her hands clasped tightly in her lap. A golden stream of sunlight flowed through the window, creating a bright puddle on the floor around them.

Adrie felt like an intruder as she crept closer, but her curiosity urged her forward until she could hear Ross's quiet prayer.

"Father, please give Nancy courage and strength. You see her situation, her need for a job, for insurance, and for a way to pay her bills. Please take care of those needs. But most of all, please help her remember that You love her and that she never has to carry this load alone. You are right here with her now and always."

Nancy sniffed. "Thank You, God. Thank You for bringing me here today. Thank You for helping me." Her choked voice barely rose above a whisper, but the message was clear. Ross's prayer meant the world to her.

A hushed reverence filled the air for a few seconds, then Ross said a quiet Amen.

Nancy lifted her head and slowly rose to her feet. "Thank you." She smiled through her tears. "I don't even know your name."

"It's Ross. Ross Peterson."

She held out her hand and clasped his. "Well, thank you, Ross. You've been God's messenger of hope for me today."

Nana walked up next to Adrie. "What's going on?" she whispered.

"Ross was just praying with that woman."

"Really?" Nana beamed. "That's wonderful."

Nancy picked up two of the books and walked toward Adrie and her grandmother. "Do you know where I can pay for these?"

"I can help you with that," Nana said.

"You know, that was real smart of you to hire that young man." Nancy nodded toward Ross as she started down the aisle with Nana. "He's got a true gift for listening and helping people."

Her grandmother nodded. "I believe he does."

Ross's dark brown eyes shone as he walked up to Adrie. "Wow, that was something else."

Adrie stared at him. "You prayed with her," she said in a hushed voice.

He shrugged and slipped his hands in his jeans pockets. "Yeah, she was pretty upset when she first came in." He lifted his gaze to meet Adrie's. "I did recommend some books. But what she really needed was someone to listen and pray."

Adrie nodded slowly as she looked from Ross to the woman at the sales counter. Maybe she had misjudged him.

Chapter Four

Adrie glanced at her watch and walked toward the front door to lock up for the evening. Her first day working with Ross hadn't been nearly as uncomfortable as she'd thought it would be. "Looks good," she said as she passed him wiping the tables in the café.

He sent her a cocky grin and lifted his hand in a salute. "Thanks. I've been slaving away all day. Glad to know I still look pretty good."

"I meant the tables, not you."

"Oh." He gave her a sad-puppy-dog face.

She shook her head and laughed. His sense of humor was corny, but he did have a way of brightening her day.

Just as she reached to flip the sign to CLOSED, the door cracked open, and an older, distinguished man with silver hair and a mustache looked inside. Adrie pulled the door open the rest of the way. "Please, come in. We'll be closing in a few minutes, but there's still time to do a little shopping if you like."

"Thank you." He glanced around the store.

"Can I help you find something?"

"Actually, I'm looking for Marian Stanton."

Adrie hesitated. Who was this man, and why did he use her grandmother's maiden name?

"Adrie, have you seen my glasses?" Nana called as she walked toward them, searching the shelves on her way. "I thought I put them beside the phone, but they seem to have taken up legs and walked off." Her words faded as she noticed the man standing with Adrie.

"Marian?" The gentleman stepped forward, a hopeful smile on his face.

Her grandmother squinted at him. "Yes? I'm sorry, I can't see too well without my glasses."

Warmth and affection radiated from his face. "It's me, Marian. George."

She gasped and raised her hand to her mouth. "George? Oh my goodness."

He moved closer and captured her hand in his. "I would've known you anywhere. You're just as lovely as ever."

Nana laughed softly and waved his compliment away. "You must need glasses just as much as I do."

Ross walked around the end of the bookcase, a hint of concern in his eyes. He leaned in close to Adrie. "Everything okay?" His warm breath fanned across her cheek.

She swallowed and squelched her reaction. "I think so."

Nana turned to them. "Adrie, Ross, this is George Bradford. He's…an old friend." She again faced George. "This is my granddaughter, Adrienne Chandler, and our new store manager, Ross Peterson."

George shook Ross's hand, then he extended his hand to Adrie. "I can definitely see the resemblance. Your grandmother looked a lot like you when we first met about fifty years ago."

Adrie shot her grandma a questioning look. She had never heard her mention George Bradford.

"So I understand it's just about closing time," George addressed Nana.

"Yes, but that's not a problem. How can we help you?"

"Well, I'd like to see your store, but to be honest, I was hoping I could invite you to dinner."

Nana's eyes widened. "Well...I'm not sure... I was just planning a simple dinner at home this evening."

"Good. Since you don't have other plans, why don't you join me? I saw a nice restaurant just down the block with outdoor seating, and it's a beautiful evening." He waited expectantly.

Nana hesitated a moment more, then her face brightened. "All right. I'll just get my purse from the office." She turned and walked away.

Adrie followed her grandmother into the office and quietly closed the door. "Grandma, who is that man?" she whispered.

"I told you, dear, his name is George Bradford. We're old friends." Nana took a hairbrush from her purse and ran it through her soft silver pageboy, checking her appearance in the small mirror beside her desk.

"Well, he certainly seems happy to see you."

"It's always a pleasure to reconnect with old friends," Nana added with a secretive smile.

"But he's taking you out to dinner. That's like a...a date."

"Yes, I suppose it is." Nana applied some lipstick, then faced Adrie. "You don't need to be concerned, dear. George was always a perfect gentleman when we dated in college."

Adrie frowned. "But I thought you dated Grandpa in college."

"I did. But I also dated George."

Adrie gasped. "At the same time?"

"Oh, no, dear. I dated George the first two years. Then he graduated and took a job in Portland. Your grandpa stayed in town and pursued me. That's how I knew he truly loved me. But George was a fine young man." Nana dropped her hairbrush into her purse. "Now, there's no reason to worry. It's just dinner with an old friend."

Adrie laid her hand on her grandmother's arm. "All right, but you haven't seen this guy for a long time. He may have changed, so be careful. Take your cell phone, and call me if you have any trouble."

Nana chuckled as she snapped her purse closed. "This is a little strange, isn't it? I'm usually the one giving you advice before you go out on a date."

Adrie followed Nana out the office door. They found Ross and George seated in the café, engaged in conversation.

George stood as Nana approached and nodded toward Ross. "You've got a fine young man managing things for you, Marian."

She nodded. "Yes, I believe we do."

"Ready to go?" He offered her his arm.

"I am." Nana slipped her hand into the crook of his elbow as though she did it every day of her life.

Adrie gripped the back of a café chair and watched her grandmother and George Bradford stroll out of the store. The bell jingled, the door closed and she turned to Ross. "I can't believe she's going out on a date with a man she hasn't seen in fifty years."

"Yeah, that's pretty cool." Ross grinned, but he quickly sobered. "What's wrong?"

Adrie bit her lip. Should she tell him? Would he understand? If she didn't say something to someone she was afraid she might burst into tears. "I'm worried about her. I don't want her to get hurt."

"George seems like a decent guy."

"But she adored my grandpa, and when he got sick and died, she was devastated." Her throat tightened, making her next words difficult. "She couldn't sleep, and she wouldn't eat. I thought I was going to lose her, too." Hot tears burned her eyes.

He stepped over and slipped his arm around her shoulder. "I'm sorry, Adrie. That must have been a difficult time for both of you." His gentle tone and caring touch sent a comforting wave through her.

She nodded and swallowed, trying to loosen her tight throat. "I miss my grandpa every day, and I thought Nana did, too." She stepped away from Ross and shuffled some papers on the sales counter.

"I'm sure she does. You can't be married that long and not miss your mate."

"Then how can she walk out the door with her old boyfriend at a moment's notice?"

Ross sent her an understanding look. "I know this is unexpected, but your grandpa's been gone for over a year. Maybe she's ready to look ahead and think about the future."

Was that true? Was her grandmother done grieving and ready to find a new love?

"It's just dinner with an old friend right now."

She nodded and pulled in a calming breath. "You're right. I don't know why I'm getting so emotional about this. He's probably just in town for the day, and nothing will come of it."

But what if she was wrong? What if her grandmother decided she didn't want to spend the rest of her life alone? Was George Bradford worthy of her grandmother's trust?

Chapter Five

Ross put the ladder away in the closet and brushed off his hands. The store was quiet this afternoon. He'd accomplished all the tasks he and Marian had planned for the day, so he grabbed a broom and headed outside. Might as well keep busy. Maybe he'd be able to greet some people, introduce himself as the new manager and invite them in.

A few minutes later, Adrie followed him out front, a bucket and scissors in her hands.

He stopped and leaned on the broom handle. "What are you going to do with those?"

"I thought I'd tend the flower boxes while you sweep. Seems like a good time to clean up things out here." Adrie trimmed off a few dead geranium blooms and dropped them in her bucket. She stuck her fingers in the dirt. "These planters seem pretty dry."

Ross glanced at the clear blue sky as he swept the last bits of leaves and dirt off the curb. "Makes sense. We haven't had any rain for a few days."

"I better haul out the hose and water them."

"I can get that for you. Where do you keep it?"

She smiled, looking pleased by his offer. "It's hanging by the side door."

"Okay. Be right back." He set his broom aside and hustled around the building. Today marked the end of his first week at the bookstore. Adrie still kept to herself most of the time, but on a few occasions he'd broken through her reserve and managed to make her smile or laugh.

Why was she so guarded? It was almost like she wore a protective coat to keep him from getting too close. But rather than repelling him, he took it as a challenge. Winning her trust and perhaps even her friendship became more important to him each day.

He lifted the hose off the metal hook and hung it over his shoulder. When he rounded the corner of the building, he saw Adrie talking with a tall man in his early thirties with short blond hair. Ross frowned and slowed his steps.

The man wore shorts and a T-shirt that showed off his muscular build. Adrie laughed at something he said and looked up at him as if he'd hung the moon.

A flash of irritation shot through Ross. Who was this guy? How come he could get that kind of reaction from her? Ross cleared his throat and tossed the hose on the sidewalk.

Adrie glanced at him, a question in her eyes.

"So are you coming to the Salmon Bake?" the man asked, ignoring Ross. "We're expecting a great turnout this year."

Adrie looked away with a shy smile. "I don't know, Eric."

Ross glared at the man as he attached the hose to the faucet and twisted it on so tight he doubted anyone would get it off.

"Come on, Adrie. It'll be fun. I'm cooking some beautiful wild king salmon fillets. Joe's Garden is donating corn on the cob. Skylark's is providing coleslaw. Avenue Bakery is sending over rolls, and Katie will be there with her cupcakes."

"Wow, you've got a great team lined up. Maybe I—"

"We're both on the schedule to work Saturday," Ross said as he handed Adrie the hose.

Eric frowned and looked him over. "And you are…?"

"Ross Peterson." He didn't offer his hand, just straightened and met Eric's steady gaze. He didn't intend to back down from the challenge in Eric's tone and stance.

Adrie sent Ross a puzzled look. "Ross, this is Eric Whittier. He's a chef at Big Fat Fish Company over on Twelfth." She turned to Eric. "Ross is our new store manager."

Eric tipped his head and shifted his gaze to Adrie, a trace of regret in his eyes. "So, you finally found a new manager. Does that mean you're leaving town to pursue your music?"

"Well, not yet." Adrie fiddled with the spray nozzle, looking flustered by his question. "I have to find a position with an orchestra first."

"But you're looking?"

She nodded. "I put the word out through friends, and I've been searching online. But it takes a while. I've known some musicians who've looked for years."

"Well, you've got talent. You'll find a spot."

"I hope so, but the competition can be pretty stiff."

"Don't worry. Something will come through for you. And in the meantime, I'll be looking for you at the Salmon Bake." He winked then backed away, still watching her.

"Thanks, Eric." She lifted her hand and waved.

Eric finally turned and sauntered off down the sidewalk.

Ross scowled at the chef. Who did he think he was coming on to her like that?

"What's wrong with you?" Adrie adjusted the spray nozzle.

"Nothing."

"Well, you're acting like your nose is out of joint just because Eric stopped to chat."

"No, I'm not." He grabbed the broom and started sweeping again even though the sidewalk looked clean.

She rolled her eyes and turned on the hose. "Okay. Whatever you say."

As soon as she turned away, he silently scolded himself for acting like a fool. He had no right to be jealous. Adrie hadn't given him any indication she was interested in him. Plus she wasn't planning to stay in Fairhaven.

And even if she was interested, what did he have to offer her? He clenched his jaw as his father's critical words rolled back through his mind. *How are you ever going to support a family? You need a more dependable career.* Maybe his father was right. All he had was an empty bank account, a small apartment and an uncertain future. Why would Adrie be interested in him?

But as he turned and watched her water the flower boxes with a trace of a smile on her full lips, everything in him wished things were different and she would give him a chance.

Chapter Six

Adrie took her flute apart, then wiped it with a soft cloth and placed it in the padded case. All around the large church sanctuary, people gathered in small groups to talk following the second worship service. Adrie quietly thought through the pastor's message, especially his final words from 1 Peter, challenging everyone to live their life entrusting themselves to God, even when things did not seem to be going well. That was a timely point, considering she hadn't found one open orchestra position since she had started her search two weeks earlier.

"Adrie, look who's here," her grandmother called as she walked toward the platform with Ross in tow.

Her stomach fluttered. She squelched her response and straightened to face him.

He was dressed in jeans and a pale yellow button-down shirt. He sent her a self-conscious grin. "Morning, Adrie."

She nodded. "Hello, Ross."

"You sounded great today, all of you." He motioned toward the six members of the worship team still on the platform. Two were putting away their instruments while the others greeted friends.

"Thanks." She snapped her flute case closed.

Geoff Swenson, the leader of their worship team, walked over and said hello to Marian. She introduced him to Ross. "So, are you new to Grace Chapel?" Geoff asked.

"I've been coming for a few months." Ross pointed to the guitar Geoff held in his hand. "Is that a Taylor?"

Geoff grinned and nodded. "Do you play?"

"A little," Ross said with a slight shrug.

"You want to try it?"

Ross looked up. "You wouldn't mind?"

"Not at all." Geoff held out the instrument to him.

Ross accepted it with reverent hands then gently ran his finger over the wood. "It's a beauty."

"Wait till you play it." Geoff stood back and smiled.

Ross slipped the strap over his head and strummed the strings. "Nice."

Adrie stilled as she watched him. Surprise rippled through her. Ross was a guitarist?

Geoff listened to Ross play for a few minutes. When Ross paused, Geoff asked, "Do you read music?"

Ross nodded. "I took piano when I was younger, then I switched to guitar about five years ago."

"Can you play this?" Geoff flipped the sheets of music to the first song they'd played in the morning service.

Adrie clutched her flute case handle. Why was Geoff asking Ross to play one of their songs?

Ross strummed through the song with perfect timing and style. When the final chord faded away, he looked up. "Nice song. It's new for me, but I really like it."

Geoff's eyebrows rose. "You've never heard it before?"

"Just when you played it in the service this morning."

"I'm impressed you could pick it up that fast." Geoff glanced around at the other team members, and then back at Ross. "Would you like to play with us?"

Adrie stifled a gasp. *What in the world!*

Ross cocked his head. "You mean on Sunday mornings?"

Geoff nodded. "We're losing one of our guitarists when he heads back to college this week. I've been praying, asking the Lord to send us someone else. Looks like you might be an answer to prayer."

Adrie cleared her throat. "Don't people usually have to fill out an application and audition?"

Geoff shot her a questioning glance. "Sure." He turned to Ross. "Why don't you stop by the church office before you leave today and pick up an application. Fill that out and bring it back on Thursday night. We practice here at seven o'clock. Can you make it this week?"

Ross nodded. "I get off at six, so that shouldn't be a problem."

"Good. That'll give you a chance to meet everyone. Bring a song to play, and then I'll give you a couple others you can play with us. How does that sound?"

Ross smiled and held out his hand to Geoff. "Great. Thanks."

Geoff chuckled. "You're welcome."

Adrie stared at Geoff and swallowed hard. Everywhere she went the response to Ross was the same. Nana thought he was their conquering hero at the bookstore and could do no wrong. All the Bayside Treasure ladies were gaga over him. Whenever they came in, they hovered around him like bees in a flower garden. And now Geoff was giving him a free pass to join the worship team.

She grabbed her flute case and strode down the steps. This was too much.

Five minutes later Adrie climbed in the car to wait for her grandmother. Glancing out the passenger window, she spotted Marian crossing the church parking lot, her head down and her steps determined.

Adrie's stomach twisted, and she sank lower in the seat. *Oh, Lord, I am about to get an earful, and I probably deserve it.*

Nana pulled open the car door, slid into the driver's seat and took the keys from her purse. Rather than starting the car, she dropped her hand to her lap and turned to Adrie. "Honey, you know I love you, but I don't understand what's going on."

"What do you mean?"

Nana tipped her head, not fooled by Adrie's questions. "It's obvious you weren't happy about Geoff inviting Ross to play with the worship team."

"Geoff doesn't even know Ross. If I hadn't said something, he would've let him skip the whole tryout process. That's not right."

"Maybe not, but it's your attitude that concerns me."

"My attitude?"

"Yes. Don't you see? If Ross can use his musical talents here at church, it might help him get connected and grow spiritually."

"But what about all the other people who'd love to play with us on Sunday mornings? Is it fair to bring someone on the team who is so new to the church?"

Nana's expression softened. "Is that really what's bothering you?"

Adrie shrugged, feeling more miserable by the minute. Where were all these conflicting feelings about Ross coming from? "I just don't understand why everyone is treating him like he's been our friend for years."

"What's wrong with that?"

"Well, it's not true. We've only known him for a couple weeks."

"But he has an engaging personality and a wonderful way with people. And that makes you feel like you've known him much longer."

"See, that's what I mean. *You* love him. *Everyone* loves him."

"And that's a problem for you because...?"

She drummed her fingers on the passenger door. Why did it bother her so much? What was really behind all this?

"Honestly, Adrie, you should be welcoming Ross with open arms. He's doing a wonderful job taking over as manager. He spent a good deal of his free time getting that new inventory system up and running, something that would've been impossible for me. He's not too proud to sweep the sidewalk or climb up ladders to change lightbulbs. I appreciate that, and you should, too."

Adrie laid her head back and sighed. "I suppose you're right. But I just can't shake these doubts I have about him."

Her grandma pursed her lips and leveled her gaze at Adrie. "I wonder if this has more to do with you feeling replaced by Ross than with him fitting in so well."

Her breath caught in her throat. Could that be true? Was she feeling threatened by the way he'd swept in and taken over so many areas of her life?

"Perhaps you're even a little jealous of him?"

"Jealous?" She shook her head, but the statement pierced her heart.

"Well, every time I praise him for doing well at the bookstore, you roll your eyes. And look what just happened with Geoff."

Was jealousy at the root of her struggle?

"Adrie, honey, listen to me. I believe God sent Ross to us. His personality and talents are a gift. Soon he'll be ready to take over the store for me, and you'll be free to go pursue your music. Isn't that what you want?"

The question hung in the air as Adrie rubbed her forehead. Was her grandmother right? Had she been looking at Ross as a competitor rather than a blessing?

Another thought struck, chilling her heart and peeling away another layer of her defenses.

Would anyone care if she left?

Closing her eyes, she blew out a deep breath. That was

it—the truth of this torment. She was afraid Ross would replace her and no one would care when she finally left Fairhaven.

Adrie slid into a booth at Dos Padres across from her friend Rachel Clark. "So how are the wedding plans coming?"

"Pretty well. Only twelve days to go. I'm just making the final calls to confirm things with people and finishing up a few details for the reception."

Scanning the menu, Adrie asked, "Is there anything I can do to help?" Though her own wedding plans had been scrapped, she'd spent months poring over magazines and websites planning her ill-fated wedding. She'd also been a bridesmaid for three of her friends, so she knew all the work and planning involved. This time she wasn't in the bridal party, but Rachel had asked her to play for their ceremony.

"Tomorrow night we're working on favors and some of the decorations for the reception, if you're free."

"Sure. I can come by after six. How does that sound?"

"Perfect. Thanks." Rachel studied her menu for a minute, then looked up. "Say, how are things going with Ross Peterson?"

Adrie's stomach tensed. "Well, he's only been with us for about three weeks."

Rachel scrutinized her, then tipped her head. "What are you not telling me?"

"Nothing." Adrie unfolded her napkin and placed it in her lap, avoiding Rachel's inquisitive gaze. "He's good with customers and helpful with the technical side of things. My grandma can't stop singing his praises."

"But what about you? You're the one who has to feel confident leaving the store in his hands. What do you think of him?"

She pressed her lips together. Rachel's fiancé, Cam, was

good friends with Ross. She'd need to be careful about her comments, but she owed her friend an honest answer. "He seems to have a good handle on the job, and he can certainly be charming when the mood strikes. But he still wants to pursue photography on the side, and that makes me wonder if I'm going to invest a lot of time and effort training him, then he'll walk out and leave us stranded."

Rachel shook her head. "Ross wouldn't do that. He's very dependable. Cam thinks the world of him. Did I tell you that he asked Ross to be his best man?"

"I thought Matt Larson was the best man."

"He is, but Cam asked Ross first. He said he was hoping to be our wedding photographer." Rachel leaned across the table and lowered her voice. "He's not even charging us. Can you believe it? That is such a huge gift."

Adrie leaned forward. "Wow, that's certainly generous."

Rachel smiled and nodded. "He's an awesome photographer. We're thrilled. Most photographers charge two to three thousand dollars. Of course we told him that we'd pay for developing all the photos. He's had a rough time since he had to close his studio, so we couldn't let him pay for that, especially after everything he's done for us."

"You mean besides the wedding photography?"

Rachel nodded. "He took our engagement photos and wouldn't let us pay for those, either. He's always helping Cam with painting and repair jobs at the house." Rachel laughed softly. "You should see them. There's nothing those two like better than swinging a hammer or running a circular saw."

Adrie frowned slightly. "Sounds like he's been a good friend."

"The best," Rachel said. "I think you've finally found someone you can depend on to manage the bookstore. I'm sure he won't let you down like those other guys you hired."

The words on the menu blurred before Adrie's eyes. Was

Rachel right? Could she trust Ross? Three weeks didn't seem long enough to judge a man's character and integrity or to know if he was going to stick around and do the job.

Troubling questions swirled through her mind. Was Ross the right person to take over her job? Was that what she truly wanted—someone stepping in and filling her shoes, enjoying the life and relationships she'd built for herself in Fairhaven?

If she was going to follow her dream, that was what it would take—giving it all up for the sake of her music. Was she willing to pay that price? And if she did, would it fill that empty void in her heart?

Adrie carried the box of fall decorations up the basement steps and set it on the sales counter. It was time to change the window display and decorate the store for the new season. The temperature had been dropping at night, and the leaves would start changing soon.

The bell over the front door jingled. Irene, Barb and Hannah trooped in, chattering like a flock of birds. Adrie smiled and glanced at her watch. Three o'clock, Monday afternoon. Time for the Bayside Treasures to meet.

"Hello, Adrie honey." Irene crossed the store and gave her a big hug. "Oh, you look so pretty today. I love that green sweater. It's the perfect color for you. Is it new?"

Adrie smiled. "No, but it's one of my favorites."

"I can see why. It looks lovely on you." Irene set her container of cookies on a café table then glanced around. "Is Marian in the office?"

"Yes. You can go on back." Adrie greeted Barb and Hannah while Irene went to fetch Nana.

Barb slipped behind the café counter and poured herself a cup of coffee. "How's the job hunt going? Any news?"

Adrie shook her head. "I was looking online and saw an opening in Atlanta, but when I contacted them, they said their flutist changed her mind and decided to stay." She pulled a box cutter from her pocket and carefully slit the packing tape on the box of decorations.

Hannah clicked her tongue. "Well, we'll just have to double up our prayers."

"That's right. God knows what you need—just one opening. Then as soon as you audition, I know they'll snap you up." Barb took a sip and looked at Adrie over the rim of her coffee mug. "You are keeping up with your practice schedule, aren't you? You want to be in top form when the call finally comes."

"I'm trying. But I've got practice for the worship team, and I've been spending a lot of time training Ross, plus I've been helping Rachel get ready for her wedding."

"Did I hear my name?" Ross walked past Adrie, then stopped at the community bulletin board to pin up a concert poster.

Hannah chuckled. "That's right. We're talking about you."

"Good things, I hope." He grinned, winking at Adrie, his dark eyes dancing with humor.

Her face flushed. She looked down and fumbled with the flaps on the box. Why was she so flustered by that little wink? He didn't mean anything by it, did he?

"Here let me help you with that." Ross held the flaps open while she reached in for a strand of silk fall leaves.

"Thanks." Her hand brushed his, and a shiver raced along her arm. She stopped and looked up. Her gaze connected with Ross, her pulse pounding out a steady beat.

He searched her face, and his smile dissolved into a concerned look. "What's wrong?"

She jerked her gaze away, her face flaming. "Nothing."

He stepped around the box and into her line of vision. "You sure?" He kept his voice low, but she could feel Barb and Hannah watching them.

She didn't dare look him in the eye, so she focused on untangling the strand of leaves. "Yes, I'm just…feeling a little stressed about the job hunt, I guess."

"How come? Something going on that you haven't told me about?" His tone was light, but she could hear the concern in his voice.

Before she could tell him more, her grandmother strolled into the café with Irene. "Sorry to keep you ladies waiting." She grinned and waved some small tickets in the air. "Look what I have."

Hannah squinted at Nana as she settled into a chair. "What's that?"

"Two complimentary tickets to the Salmon Bake on Saturday. Who wants to go with me?"

Irene sent Nana a wistful look. "I love salmon, but I just started my new diet, and that would be way too tempting."

"I can't go. I'm allergic to all seafood," Barb said.

"How about you, Hannah? Are you free on Saturday?"

"Sorry, I promised my sister, Val, I'd drive down to Everett to see her and her husband."

Suddenly, a bright smile broke over Irene's face. "I know, why don't you give the tickets to Ross and Adrie? I bet they'd like to go."

Nana spun around. "What a great idea! Why didn't I think of that?"

Adrie's stomach clenched, and she took a step back. "Wait, I thought you were looking for someone to go with you."

"Oh, that's okay. I go every year."

"But I'm scheduled to work on Saturday, and so is Ross. We can't leave you here all by yourself."

"I'll come in and help," Barb said with a smug smile.

"Me, too," Irene added with wide innocent eyes. "No need for you kids to miss out on all the fun."

Adrie twisted the strand of silk fall leaves around her fingers.

"It's a wonderful event. They cook the corn and the salmon right there on the Village Green. You can have a nice little picnic in the center of town." Nana looked at her with a hopeful expression.

Ross cocked his head and smiled at Adrie. "I'm game, if you are."

She bit her lip. The Salmon Bake did sound fun, but she wasn't sure about spending that much one-on-one time with Ross. She was trying not to think of him as a threat, but now she was more concerned about the unsettling attraction she felt toward him.

His hopeful expression dimmed. "That's okay. If you don't want to go, I understand."

"It's not that, it's just..." What? She couldn't think of an excuse that made sense, not with everyone else standing around staring at them, holding their breath.

"It would be good PR for Ross to get out there and meet some of the other business owners. You could introduce him," Nana added.

"I suppose that's true."

"It would be a shame to let the tickets go to waste." Ross rubbed his chin. "I guess I could find someone else who'd like to go."

Surprise shot through Adrie. He would ask someone else? Who? She straightened and met his gaze. "Well, I suppose it would be okay as long as Barb and Irene can cover for us."

Ross's face brightened. "So you'll go?"

She pulled in a shaky breath. "Sure. It's important for people to see that Bayside Books supports community events."

The ladies all broke out in smiles. Irene clapped, and Hannah gave Nana's arm a pat.

Adrie sighed and rolled her eyes.

"Here you go." Marian passed them each a ticket.

"Are you sure? Saturday is usually our busiest day."

"We'll be fine. You two go, have some fun together. Take the whole afternoon off."

"Okay. Thanks." Adrie forced a small smile. Nana had good intentions, though it was clear she and her friends were still hoping to play matchmaker.

Nana joined the other ladies at the table, and they set up their Scrabble game. Adrie pulled a basket of artificial gourds and mini pumpkins out of the decoration box.

Ross stepped up next to her. "Don't look so worried. I promise it'll be a fun day."

A shiver raced up her arm again. That was exactly what she was afraid of.

Chapter Seven

Adrie looped the soft lavender scarf around her neck and checked her appearance in her bedroom mirror. The color was great, but was it too much? Did it make her look like she was trying too hard? Closing her eyes, she tried to regain her focus.

This was not a date. She was just going to the Salmon Bake with Ross.

Then why were her emotions getting so tangled up? She would be leaving Fairhaven soon, so there was no sense in even thinking about getting involved with Ross or anyone else.

A thump sounded on the other side of the wall, and she stepped back. What was Ross doing over there? He was usually so quiet she didn't even know when he was home. But since they'd come upstairs to get ready, he'd been bumping around in what she thought must be his bedroom closet. She had been in that apartment many times to help her grandma clean and paint between renters, and that seemed to be where the sound was coming from.

She took one more look in the mirror then turned away. There was no need to redo her makeup or change her outfit. She grabbed her purse off the bed, but then she turned around and she headed into the bathroom. Even though this wasn't an official date, she shouldn't go out the door looking like she didn't care how she looked.

She ran a brush through her hair, then added blush, mascara and a touch of lip gloss. At least that gave her some color and made her look presentable.

The knock at her door set her heart pounding. "You are being ridiculous," she whispered as she walked to the door. When she pulled it open, Ross greeted her with a smile. He now wore comfortable jeans and a forest-green V-neck sweater that looked great with his olive-toned skin. Over his shoulder he carried his black leather camera bag.

"Are you ready to go?" he asked, his expression warm and open.

She nodded and sent him a tight-lipped smile. "All set."

"Okay." He led the way down the steps. She followed.

They set off walking toward the center of town. She bit her lip, trying to think of a good topic for conversation. But it had been so long since she had gone out with anyone besides Adam, she felt stumped. Of course there had been that one disastrous blind date with Irene's friend Noah. She shuddered.

But this wasn't a date, so she didn't need to worry. Right?

Ross glanced over at her. "Have you been to the Salmon Bake before?"

"No."

"Salmon is one of my favorites. Do you like seafood?"

"Yes." She looked away. Why did she suddenly feel so nervous and tongue-tied? She and Ross had worked together almost one month.

They walked another half block in silence.

"I brought my camera." He tapped the bag he carried on his shoulder. "Thought I might take some photos."

"Of what?"

"Anything and everything." He grinned at her, and she

couldn't help returning a small smile. "You never know what we might see at an event like this. Maybe I'll get lucky."

"Lucky? What do you mean?"

"If I get a great shot, I might be able to sell it to *The Bellingham Herald* or *Entertainment Northwest*."

"Have you sold photos to the paper before?"

"A few. They usually send out their own photographers. But if I capture something special, I can send it over and see if they want it. And there are a couple of websites looking for photos of local events."

"What's your favorite type of thing to photograph?"

That kept Ross talking for several minutes as he told her how he enjoyed shooting sunsets on Bellingham Bay or the trails and bridge at Whatcom Falls. But his favorites were the majestic peaks of Mount Baker, Mount Shuksan and Picture Lake.

Adrie slowly relaxed as she listened and before she knew it, they rounded the corner and arrived at the Village Green. She was thankful for the bustling crowd gathered there. With all the noise and activity, she wouldn't have to be the sole focus of Ross's attention.

Grills and serving tables had been set up beneath the pergola along one side of the square. A line of people waiting to pick up their meal stretched to the far end of the green. Up on the stage, a four-member band played a country western song. People sat on the grass in groups, listening to the music and enjoying their plates piled high with salmon, corn on the cob, coleslaw and rolls. Some people were already enjoying cupcakes for dessert.

"Wow. It smells great," Ross said. "Let's get in line." He placed his hand on the small of her back and guided her through the crowd.

Adrie was initially surprised by his touch, but the warmth of his hand felt comforting and protective. They found a place at the end of the line. He dropped his hand, and she found herself missing his touch. *Honestly, Adrie, what is the matter with you? Are you so desperate you'd assign romantic intentions to that simple touch? He's just being a gentleman.*

"Adrie! Good to see you," a male voice called.

She spotted Eric waving a long-handled spatula from behind the barbecue grill.

She lifted her hand halfway. "Hi, Eric. How's it going?"

"Great! Good thing you came now. We're going to sell out soon." He set down his spatula and came around the end of the grill. "Come with me, and I'll get you a plate."

Adrie's face flushed as she pointed over her shoulder at Ross. "Thanks, but we've got tickets."

"Oh, okay." Eric's eager smile faded. "Well, enjoy your meal." With a disappointed shrug, he returned to his spot behind the grill.

Adrie fiddled with the scarf at her neck, trying to let in some cool air. She hadn't promised Eric she would meet him here. Still, she didn't like to disappoint her friend.

"How long have you known Eric?"

"Oh…three or four years."

Ross sent her a questioning glance, obviously wanting to know more.

"We went to college together. He dated my roommate, Celia, most of my senior year."

Ross lifted one dark eyebrow. "Looks like he wishes he'd dated you."

"That would never have worked. I was dating Adam at the time." Her face flamed.

"Adam?"

She swallowed. "My ex-fiancé."

He cocked his head. "You were engaged? What happened?" As soon as he asked, he lifted his hand. "Sorry. That's none of my business."

She hesitated. Did she want to tell him the details? It

would mean admitting the humiliating truth—he'd never truly loved her. That painful reality seemed to echo through her whole life, underlying so many of her relationships.

Those disappointments and betrayals had chilled her heart and pushed her further away from the free-spirited, loving woman she wanted to be. Adam's unfaithfulness was just one more painful wound that fortified the wall around her heart.

"You don't have to tell me if you'd rather not," Ross said, his voice gentle.

"No, it's okay." She lifted her gaze to meet his. "Adam and I met in college during our sophomore year when we played in the orchestra together. We dated for the next two years, and then, right after graduation, he proposed. We were supposed to get married last month, but in April, after most of our wedding plans were already made, I found out he was cheating on me with my former best friend."

Ross grimaced. "Oh, that's terrible." A fierce glint lit his eyes. "I'm sorry he hurt you, but I'm glad you didn't marry him. You deserve better than that."

His sincere words warmed her heart. But then a chill swept them away. He assumed Adam and Marie were at fault. But that wasn't the whole story. She had refused to be intimate with Adam while they were engaged. Had that pushed him into the arms of another woman? A new wave of sorrow flowed in.

"When was the wedding supposed to be?" Ross asked, bringing her back from those unhappy memories.

"September 6," she whispered, barely able to say the date.

He cocked his head. "Isn't that Marian's birthday?"

She nodded, regretting that choice all over again. "I thought it would be a nice way to honor her." Instead, it would always be a painful reminder of Adam's betrayal.

Ross rubbed his chin, his gaze still resting on her. "So the day you and I met, was the day you were supposed to marry Adam. Interesting." A slow smile lifted one side of his mouth. "Maybe that was God's way of showing you when He closes one door, He opens another."

Adrie looked up at him. What did he mean by that?

He grinned at her, his dark eyes glowing. But then something behind her captured his attention. "Hold on. Photo op." He pulled out his camera. "Would you hang on to my camera bag for a minute?"

"Sure." She slipped it over her shoulder. "What are you going to take a picture of?"

"See that man with his son?" He made a couple quick adjustments to his camera, then lifted it to his eye and clicked off a series of shots. "That's the kind of photo my friend at the *Herald* would love."

The dad lifted up his young son on his shoulders and gave him a wild ride that had them both laughing. The little boy placed his hands over his dad's eyes. The father played along, pretending he was blind, and staggered around to the delight of his giggling son.

Adrie smiled as she watched them, then her gaze shifted to Ross.

He crouched to get a different angle for his next photo. "Save my place. I've got to get their names." He walked over and introduced himself. Then he pulled a small notepad from his back pocket and jotted down their information.

The line inched ahead slowly. It looked like it would be a few minutes before they got their food, but Adrie didn't mind. She tapped her foot in time to the song played by the band, while the tantalizing scent of the grilled salmon and roasting corn drifted toward her, making her mouth water. Warm sunshine on her shoulders eased the tightness in her neck and back.

As she watched Ross, the truth settled in her heart. She was enjoying spending the afternoon with him. He'd surprised her again with his sense of humor and his caring words and actions. She would've missed it all if she'd followed her first impulse and said no to her grandmother's pleas. And that would've been a foolish mistake.

Ross glanced at his watch as he and Adrie walked back toward the bookstore. It was only three forty-five. He didn't want to say goodbye to her yet, especially now that she finally seemed to be enjoying herself. He shot off a quick prayer, and within seconds, an idea formed in his mind. He sent his silent thanks heavenward.

"Have you ever been up to Marys Peak?" He shifted the strap of the camera bag and glanced her way. "Les Hawkins was telling me about it the other day. He said there's a great view from up there."

"Les Hawkins, our mailman?" She sent him a quizzical look, but a slight smile teased the corners of her mouth.

He nodded. "He thought it might be a good place to take photos."

Adrie's smile spread wider, and she broke out in soft laughter.

"What's so funny?"

"You are."

"What did I do now?"

"I can't believe the way you make friends so easily. You just met Les. He comes in the store no more than five minutes a day, but you've already made a connection with him. And it's not just Les, everywhere we go, people seem drawn to you."

He lifted his hands. "What can I say? I like people."

"And they seem to like you."

He chuckled. "You think so?"

"Yes, I do." Her sunny mood seemed to dim a little. "It's probably because you have such an easygoing personality." Her brows dipped as though that was a problem.

"Thanks—I think."

"I meant it as a compliment." She bit her lip and kicked a stray stone across the sidewalk. "Don't get me wrong. That's a good quality, but…"

"But what?"

"I guess I wish I was more like that."

He slowed his steps. "Why would you say that? People like you just the way you are."

She turned to him with a skeptical glance. "Really?"

"Sure. Look at Eric. He likes you." His tone was teasing, but he hoped she might explain if there was something going on between them.

"Well, I am not interested in him."

"No? Why not?" he asked, keeping his tone light.

"I'm just not, that's all." She picked up the pace again.

He easily matched her steps, hoping he wasn't making a mistake by pushing this subject a little further. "He seems like a decent guy."

Her cheeks flushed. "I don't want to get involved with Eric…or anyone else. It wouldn't make sense, not when I'm probably leaving town." Her voice trembled slightly, and she shifted her gaze away.

They walked on in silence for a few seconds and he pondered her words. She seemed to be giving him clear warning that she was not available. But that probably had more to do with her former fiancé's betrayal and her wounded heart than the future demands of her music career.

Should he heed that warning and save himself the possible heartache, or try to break through that wall around her heart? His glance shifted to Adrie. She stared straight ahead with a determined tilt to her chin. But there was a vulnerable look in her eyes, as though she was just waiting to see if he would take her words at face value and keep his distance. She might be cool and even a bit prickly on the outside, but underneath there was a warm and loving woman worth pursuing.

But was he the man who should be pursuing her?

Bright morning sunshine filtered through the front windows, adding a warm glow to the bookstore's interior. Adrie sat on the tall wooden stool behind the sales counter and picked up the latest copy of *Christian Retailing* magazine. Thumbing through the first few pages, she glanced at the headlines, but her gaze kept drifting toward Ross. He sat a few feet away with his eyes glued to the computer screen, his hands hovering over the keys. He hadn't said a word to her in at least twenty minutes.

She cleared her throat. "How's it coming?"

He didn't look up, and a few seconds passed before he spoke. "I'm just checking it over now." He frowned, scrolled down the page, and typed in a few more things.

She leaned to the left, trying to see the rest of the screen, but his broad shoulders blocked her view. She sat back. He needed to learn how to place orders without her help. But she had a hard time resisting the urge to check his work.

The revenue from their December sales had to carry them through the first few months of the next year. Having the right stock on hand made all the difference between profit and loss. She drummed her fingers on the counter. "Did you add in those Christmas cards we talked about yesterday?"

"Yep."

"How about the calendars?"

"Got 'em." He continued to stare at the computer screen.

She pulled in a slow deep breath and focused on the magazine again. She needed to relax and let him do it. That was the only way he would get the experience he needed to run the store. And she couldn't leave until she was certain he could handle the job.

A pang shot through her heart as she thought of saying

goodbye to everyone she loved. Was that what she truly wanted—to leave her grandmother, her job, her church, her friends? Her gaze shifted to Ross again, and the pain cut deeper. Though she had only known him for a few weeks, they were developing a connection she couldn't deny.

Closing her eyes, she pushed those troubling questions away.

She could not change course now. For fourteen years she had carried one dream in her heart, and she couldn't imagine any other future. If she wanted to play professionally, she could not stay in Fairhaven. The only orchestra nearby was the Whatcom Symphony. They were a wonderful group, but the musicians were all volunteers. They only played part-time and had to support themselves with other jobs or have spouses who carried that burden.

If she was going to establish her career and support herself, she would have to spread her wings and leave Fairhaven behind. That was the sacrifice she would have to make, so why were these doubts filling her mind now?

Another question burrowed deeper into her heart, stealing her breath away. What if she wasn't good enough? What if no one wanted to hire her after all the years of work she had put in? What would she do then?

Was that what was really bothering her, or did her hesitation have more to do with the man sitting just a few feet away? Was she willing to give up the possibility of something developing with Ross?

"What do you think about these Christmas novella collections?" Ross asked, still focused on the screen.

She blinked and struggled to find her voice. "The price is good, especially if you order the display set."

She slid off her stool and stood behind him. "The historical collections usually sell better than the contemporaries." Leaning over his shoulder, she checked the ordering information on the screen. A warm, woodsy scent floated in the air around him. She pulled in a slow deep breath to steady herself, but that just intensified the delicious scent.

He reached for his coffee and took a drink, but he didn't look her way. "Okay. I'll add those to the order."

Frustration zinged through her nerves. Why was he so focused and businesslike today? Where was the lighthearted banter they usually enjoyed?

She sat on the stool again, her spirit sinking lower. What did she expect? She was the one who told him that she didn't want to get involved with Eric or anyone—namely him. Talk about squelching a guy's hopes. But what else could she say? She needed to maintain her distance so neither of them got hurt. That was the right decision...wasn't it?

Her stomach twisted into a sour knot. She rubbed her forehead, trying to ease the pounding over her eyebrows. She needed to take a break before she said or did something she would regret. "I'm going to make some chai." She stood and walked around the counter.

The bell over the front door jingled. George Bradford stepped in and glanced around the store. Spotting Adrie and Ross, he lifted his hand and waved to them.

A flash of concern shot through Adrie. She had hoped Nana's old beau might only be in town for a short time, but it looked like this was either a long visit or a permanent move.

A slight wave of guilt washed over her. She wanted her grandmother to be happy, truly she did. And reconnecting with George had certainly lifted her grandmother's spirits.

"Morning, Adrie. Ross." George's gaze traveled around the store. "Is Marian in?"

Ross stood. "Sorry, George, she's not here right now." He glanced at Adrie, silently asking if they should tell him more.

She nodded, thankful he picked up on her concern.

"She's getting a haircut," Ross added.

"When do you expect her back?"

"Not until later this afternoon."

He nodded slowly. "Well, perhaps I could write her a note."

"Sure." Ross took pad of paper and pen from the back counter. "Here you go."

George's eyes lit up, and he pointed to Ross's camera sitting on the counter by the computer. "That looks like a nice Canon."

"It is." Ross picked it up and held it out to George. "Sounds like you know your cameras."

George chuckled. "That's been my business for almost forty years." He lifted the camera to his eye and adjusted the focus. "In fact, that's why I came back to Fairhaven."

Ross cocked his head. "What do you mean?"

George handed the camera back. "My sister, Claudia, and her husband, Ray, own Clarkson's Photography over on Harris Street. Ray has some health issues that are slowing him down, and since I'm retired, they asked if I could come out and keep the studio running for a few months while Ray is on the mend."

So this wasn't just a short visit, Adrie noted.

"I've seen some of Ray's photos," Ross said. "He's a very talented guy."

"You're familiar with Ray's work?"

Ross nodded. "I had my own photo studio for a couple years. I still do some work on the side."

"Is that right? Well, no wonder you have such a nice camera."

Ross grinned and walked around the sales counter. "Would you like a cup of coffee, George?"

"As a matter of fact, I would. Thanks." He patted Ross on the shoulder, and they walked toward the café discussing the latest lens Ross has purchased for his camera.

It looked like Ross had found a way to connect with George. No surprise there. But would all this talk about photography draw Ross away from his commitment to the bookstore? How long would George be in town? Would he and her grandmother remain friends, or was he hoping for something more?

Chapter Eight

Ross grabbed a bale of hay out of the trunk of his car and turned to Adrie. "Where do you want this?" The twine cut into his hands as he waited for her answer, but he didn't mind. This was a chance to help her with a project that seemed important to her.

Yesterday morning she'd called him over to the computer and told him about the scarecrow contest among the business owners in Fairhaven's historic district.

Scrolling down the page, she pointed out photos of her favorites from last year's contest. "If we have a prize-winning scarecrow this time, they'll put it in the paper, which gives us some free publicity and possibly some new customers."

Ross hoped she was right. Marian had called him in the office last night just before closing to tell him sales were running significantly lower than last year. She hoped things would pick up with the approaching holidays. She asked him to pray they did.

But what if sales didn't improve? Would he be job-hunting again by New Year's? He'd never get his photo studio up and running again if he didn't hold on to this job and build up his savings account.

"Ross, can you bring that hay over here?" Adrie called.

She set a black plastic trash bag on the sidewalk next to the bookstore's front entry where she'd already arranged two large pumpkins, several gourds and some colorful mum plants in bright autumn colors.

Ross lowered the hay bale to the sidewalk and wiped his hands on his jeans. "What's in there?" He nodded to the trash bag.

She smiled up at him. "Everything we need to make our prize-winning scarecrows."

He chuckled. "Let's see what you've got."

She reached in and pulled out an old pair of denim overalls and a broad-brimmed straw hat. "I'm thinking we want a traditional harvest look, but with our own creative touch." She set aside the hat and overalls and pulled out two small folding beach chairs and a red-and-white-striped beach umbrella.

He nodded toward the umbrella. "That should get people's attention."

"I hope so. I want to impress the judges, but I also want people to stop and take a look."

He couldn't help smiling as he watched her. Lately she seemed happier and more relaxed. The faint lines around her eyes and mouth had faded, and the healthy glow on her cheeks made her more attractive than ever. He shifted his gaze away, determined to stay focused on the project. "So what's the plan?"

"I thought we'd make a guy and a girl scarecrow seated side by side, reading books." She took a sign from the bag that read *A Harvest of Great Reading at Bayside Books.* "What do you think?"

"I like it, but what's going to make ours stand out from all the rest?"

"The way we dress them, of course." With a lighthearted grin, she took out a red plaid flannel shirt, a navy-blue bandanna, a pair of old hiking boots and a rubber mask that looked like an old man's face.

"I'm not sure that fits your happy harvest theme." Ross pointed to the mask. "It's more a haunted house look."

"Really?" She studied the mask. "Maybe when we dress him and add this cute hat and sunglasses he'll look more like Farmer Brown than Freddy Krueger."

Ross chuckled. "Do you have one of those masks for Mrs. Brown?"

"As a matter of fact, I do." She sent him another teasing grin and pulled out a Marilyn Monroe rubber face mask.

He whistled. "That'll stop traffic."

She gave his shoulder a playful shove. "I should've known you'd say that."

"Who could resist that come-hither look in her eyes?" He grinned and wiggled his eyebrows.

She snorted and shook her head. "You're too funny."

So much for his attempt at flirting.

Working together, they stuffed the first scarecrow's body and seated him in the chair. Adrie filled the mask and attached it to Farmer Brown's neck, while Ross knelt and shoved the scarecrow's legs into the old boots. Adrie tied the kerchief around the scarecrow's neck, added the sunglasses and placed the hat on his head at a jaunty angle.

Ross stood, and his gaze slid from the scarecrow to Adrie. A gentle breeze blew a few strands of her fiery auburn hair around her face. She lifted her hand and gracefully brushed them away. Tilting her head, she surveyed her creation. "What do you think?"

Her slim brown corduroys and soft peach sweater accented her trim figure and attractive curves. She was nothing short of… "Beautiful," he murmured. Had he actually said that out loud?

She turned and sent him a quizzical look, a slight smile lifting the corners of her mouth. "What did you say?"

Fire flashed up his neck. "Best scarecrow I've ever seen." He snatched the pair of work gloves off the pile and knelt on the sidewalk. "But he still needs his gloves."

"Okay." Her voice still held a question.

He could feel beads of sweat forming on his forehead as he fumbled with the gloves. "How are we going to get him to hold the book?"

"Maybe we could use rubber bands." Adrie knelt beside him, holding the scarecrow's arm still while he tugged on the gloves. "If we set the book in his lap, I can wrap the rubber bands around it and slip the thumbs of his gloves under." She glanced at him, her eyes wide, waiting for his response.

She was only inches away now, close enough he could see a faint dusting of pale freckles across her nose and the dark sweep of lashes around her amazing eyes. The sweet scent of flowers and sunshine drew him closer. If he leaned down he could kiss her. But a warning pulsed through him. If he crossed that line now, he would destroy his chances. He forced himself to break eye contact.

What had she said? "Rubber bands. Yeah, that's a good idea."

She took a few from her pocket and secured the book to the gloves. "There. That should do it." A triumphant smile spread across her face as she rose to her feet.

Ross grabbed a handful of hay to start stuffing Mrs. Brown, but their work felt more like play as he teased Adrie, and she teased him right back. By the time they seated Mrs. Brown next to her husband, they were laughing so hard they had to stop to catch their breath.

He closed his eyes, soaking in the crazy, wonderful feelings zinging through him. How long had it been since he'd felt this alive?

"Hey, quit daydreaming." She gave his shoulder a playful shake. "We've got work to do."

His eyes flew open. "I'm not daydreaming."

"Looks like it to me." She tossed a handful of hay at him.

Grinning, he scooped up some hay and threw it back at her.

She gasped and ducked. "You missed!" Popping up, she made a silly face at him.

"Oh, no. You're not getting away with that." He grabbed her arm, pulled her closer and tickled her waist.

Laughing, she bent and tried to squirm away, but he held on tight and continued the game.

"Stop, please, stop," she gasped, still laughing.

"Not until you promise to be good. No more hay in the face."

"Okay. I promise!"

He dropped his hands and let her go. Chuckling, he leaned in closer. "I didn't know you were so ticklish."

Her laughter died. She pulled in a ragged breath. Brushing the hair away from her face, she locked gazes with him. Her pulse pounded at the base of her throat, and all the playfulness vanished from her expression. "I can't…do this…"

Her words knocked the wind out of him. "I was just playing around. I didn't mean…" But he couldn't finish his sentence. It wasn't true. He did want her in his arms, and he'd thought for a moment she wanted that, too.

With her face flaming, she spun away and stuffed the leftover clothing in the plastic bag. "I'll finish this later." She picked it up and fled around the side of the bookstore.

Stifling a moan, he kicked the pile of hay on the sidewalk. "Great!" Now he'd really done it.

Early the next morning, Adrie bent to stretch, and then adjusted the shoelaces on her running sneakers. The sound of the water lapping against the piling of the Taylor Dock created a soothing rhythm, but that did little to calm her restless thoughts.

Pulling back her hair in a ponytail, she set off jogging up the South Bay Trail. Sunlight rippled across the deep blue water of Bellingham Bay, flashing back at her like sparkling diamonds. A few small boats bobbed on the slight swells as a soft breeze fluttered their sails. Overhead, feathery clouds painted long trails across the sky.

She hoped running would clear her head. She hadn't slept well last night. In fact, she'd lain awake long past midnight while conflicting thoughts about Ross tumbled through her mind. She'd never imagined building those scarecrows together could create so much trouble. But as soon as she had let her guard down, he'd misread her playful attitude and come way too close.

Whose fault was that? If she was honest, she had to admit she'd met each one of his teasing comments and actions with a lighthearted comeback of her own. Why had she let things get so out of hand? What was she going to say the next time she saw him? How could she get things back to the way they were before that heart-racing tickling match?

Heat flashed into her cheeks at the memory of his warm breath on her neck as he'd pulled her to his chest and tickled her until she was gasping for breath and begging him to stop.

Reckless and foolish, that's what she'd been. This was not the right time to get involved with him. Even if she was staying in Fairhaven, he wouldn't be right for her. Sure he was fun and handsome, but they were so different. She was quiet and reserved—he was friendly and outgoing. She was serious and meticulous—he was lighthearted and free-spirited. She had grown up with missionary parents and had a solid faith, but he was a new believer, and he hadn't ever mentioned his family.

It would never work. She wouldn't let it. She couldn't.

Soon she'd be packing up her car and moving to a new city where she would make a fresh start with new friends who didn't know anything about her past. But when would that be? She still hadn't found any open auditions.

Lord, You promised to give us the desires of our heart if we delight in You. And You know my heart's desire has always been to play my flute professionally. I've asked You so many times, but I'm asking again. Would You please open up that door for me?

No sooner had that prayer flown from her lips than she spotted a man standing on the path about fifty yards ahead. He lifted his camera and pointed it toward the bay.

Recognition flashed through Adrie, and she slowed her steps.

Ross lowered his camera, looked her way and lifted his hand. She'd have to speak to him now. Maybe this was for the best. At least they'd have more privacy here than at the bookstore.

He watched her approach with a wary gaze. "Morning, Adrie."

Her heart sank as she noted the shadows beneath his eyes and the tired slope of his shoulders. Apparently, he hadn't slept well, either. "Hi. Are you taking pictures?" She groaned inwardly. What a lame observation.

"Yeah. Thought I might capture something special this morning since the weather's so nice."

She bit her lip. "I'm just out for a run." Another brilliant remark.

He glanced down the trail, then back at her. "I'd offer to tag along, but running with a camera might be a challenge." He tapped the long camera lens and smiled slightly, but she couldn't ignore the hint of sadness in his eyes. He seemed to be giving her a graceful exit, but that wouldn't settle the issues between them.

She mustered up her courage. "How about a walk then?"

Surprise flashed in his tired eyes. "Okay."

They set off at an easy pace, but Adrie's heart banged

in her chest like she was running a marathon. "About what happened yesterday... I think I owe you an apology."

He shook his head, and shot her an embarrassed glance. "No need to apologize."

"But I think I may have given you the wrong impression."

He frowned but didn't speak.

"The way I was playing around probably made you think that I...that I wanted..."

He held up his hand. "No, your message was loud and clear. I understand."

If he did, he was a mile ahead of her, because she was still feeling confused. But even through that confusion, she knew she had to make her boundaries clear. "I'm sorry, Ross. I can't get involved with anyone right now. I need to stay focused on my goals."

He nodded. "That makes sense. You don't have to apologize for going after your dreams. That's something I admire about you. You're determined, and you don't let your feelings get in the way."

"Right." She nodded slowly. If that was true, then why did she feel so terrible?

"So where does that leave us?"

His pointed question surprised her. "I guess..." She looked into his dark brown eyes and forced herself to say the opposite of what her heart was shouting. "I'd like to be friends."

He tipped his head and studied her. "Friends?"

She hesitated, then forced out the words. "Yes. Friends."

"You're sure?" His eyes narrowed as though reading her inner struggle.

She nodded, unable to speak past the tightness in her throat.

"Well...if that's the only choice..."

Adrie bit her lip. Was she making a mistake? It wasn't

every day you were offered a chance with someone special like Ross.

But attraction was not love. And this was attraction, pure and simple, feelings she needed to control. What mattered was following through on her plans, achieving her goals. She would not let his offer of romance or her fickle emotions derail her life plan.

Chapter Nine

Ross tossed the basketball toward the hoop and watched it bounce off the rim—again. His aim was way off today, but that was no surprise. His whole life seemed out of whack right now.

Cam snagged the rebound, dribbled around him, pivoted and shot. The ball swished through the hoop. "Yes!"

Ross blew out a disgusted breath. "That's enough for me. I quit."

"You sure? This game is really boosting my ego." Cam lifted the ball and let it fly. It swished through the hoop once more.

Ross grimaced. "Yeah. I'm sure."

Cam's triumphant grin faded. "I usually beat you, but not by this much. What's going on?"

Grabbing a towel, Ross wiped his sweaty face. Cam knew a lot about women and relationships. He'd been married for six years, then widowed, and was now engaged to be married a second time. Maybe he'd have some advice, or at least be able to commiserate. Ross lifted his eyes and met his friend's questioning gaze. "Adrie and I had the let's-just-be-friends talk this morning."

Cam frowned. "You told her that?"

Ross rolled his eyes. "No, she told me."

"Oh. Sorry." Cam bounced the ball a few more times. "I didn't know you were interested. Last thing I heard, she was giving you the iceberg treatment."

"Yeah, things warmed up a little since we started working together."

"I see." He grinned and raised one eyebrow.

"Until yesterday, that is." Ross hung the towel around his neck and sank down on the park bench.

"What happened?"

"We were goofing around, building scarecrows and I got a little physical."

"Physical how?"

"Just tickling, but it freaked her out."

Cam sent Ross a knowing nod.

"What can I say? I like her, and I was hoping something was developing between us. But I guess I was wrong."

"Just because she said she wants to be friends, that doesn't mean the door's closed."

Ross squinted at his friend. "You weren't there. Believe me. The door is not only closed, it's locked with a Do Not Disturb sign."

Cam shrugged. "So, you convince her to change her mind."

"There are a few problems with that idea."

"Such as?"

"First, her heart's set on a music career, and she doesn't think she can do that in Fairhaven."

"Yeah, Rachel mentioned that. She was worried Adrie might get a job offer and leave before the wedding."

"It hasn't happened yet, but she's ready to apply any place she finds an opening. She could end up in San Francisco, New York, London, Moscow, who knows where?"

"So? That shouldn't stop you from going after her. You've

got your job at the bookstore, but you want to get back into photography eventually, right?"

Ross nodded. "That's the plan."

"And you could do that anywhere, couldn't you?"

"Sure, but I'm Adrie's replacement. If I quit, she can't leave, at least not until she finds someone else to help her grandmother."

"Hey, with all the people out there looking for jobs, I'm sure they could find someone." Cam lifted the basketball and spun it on his finger. "That is if you two get together."

"And that's a big *if*, let me tell you."

"So, what's the other problem?"

Ross leaned back. "She was engaged before, and the guy was a real jerk. A few months before the wedding she found out he was cheating on her with her best friend."

"Wow. That hurts."

"Yeah." Ross clenched his jaw. If he ever met that guy, he'd have a hard time not punching him in the face. "She says she doesn't want to start anything because she's leaving town, but I think she's scared of getting hurt again."

"Great!" Cam's smile resurfaced and he rubbed his hands together. "That's the kind of resistance you can overcome."

"How am I supposed to do that?"

"It's just a challenge, not a closed door. She wants to be friends? Fine. You be the best friend she's ever had. Get her talking, and be a good listener. Find out her likes and dislikes. Be there when she needs you. But don't cross the line or push to make it more serious until she's ready."

"When will that be? How will I know?"

Cam grinned and his blue eyes gleamed. "Oh, you'll know. She'll tell you."

"She will?"

He nodded, resting his hand on Ross's shoulder. "But the most important thing to remember is this—if she's the one, and God's behind it, then you just need to do your part. Be the man. Pray and watch God move. But you've got to seek Him and trust Him. Do what He's telling you to do.

"You might win her heart," Cam continued, "or you might not, but if you're trusting Him and letting Him lead, you can't go wrong."

Ross nodded, letting those words sink in. "Okay. Pray, ask God to lead the way and be a world-class best friend."

Cam slapped him on the back. "You got it. That plan works every time."

Adrie snatched a tissue from the box on the coffee table and caught her explosive sneeze just in time. With a weary sigh, she dabbed at her sore nose and tossed the tissue on the growing pile on the floor by the couch. She should get up and get a trash can, but she felt so tired and achy that just the thought of moving exhausted her.

Lying back on her pillow, she let her eyes drift shut. This was a terrible time to get sick. Rachel's wedding was only three days away, and she could not let her friend down. Plus all their holiday stock was arriving at the bookstore this week. They needed to do some major rearranging before they could put those items on display.

A knock sounded at her apartment door. Adrie lifted her head and squinted toward it. Was it her grandmother? She'd called her first thing this morning, explaining she was too sick to come downstairs and work.

"Who is it?" she called, her voice sounding rough and scratchy.

"It's Ross. Can I come in?"

Adrie gasped and pulled up the blanket to her neck, covering her gray sweatpants and red T-shirt. Her hair was pulled up in a messy ponytail, and she hadn't showered since yesterday.

"I'm not feeling well," she croaked. "Go away." She

winced at how rude that sounded. "Or come back tomorrow," she added, too exhausted to think of a nicer reply.

"I know you're sick. I brought you some soup."

Soup? She flopped back on the pillow. Even though she had a runny nose and a headache, some warm soup sounded great. "Okay, come on in. It's unlocked."

The door creaked open, and Ross stepped in carrying a plastic container in one hand and a bulging plastic grocery bag in the other. He sent her a sympathetic glance. "I'd ask how you're doing, but I'm afraid it's obvious."

"Thanks."

"What I meant was, I'm sorry you're sick. It looks like you could use a little help from a friend." He set the shopping bag on her coffee table and surveyed her living room. She cringed. Her usually neat living room was strewn with mail, newspapers and a few dirty dishes on the coffee table as well as a stack of books by the couch next to her pile of used tissues.

"Would you like some soup now, or should I put it in the fridge?"

Adrie eyed the container. "What kind of soup is it?"

"Homemade chicken noodle."

"You're kidding. You made chicken soup for me?"

"Of course." He sent her a teasing grin. "Actually, your grandmother made it, so she sent me over to her house to pick it up."

Was Nana trying to play matchmaker again? Adrie narrowed her eyes and scowled at him. "Did she send you up here, or was this your idea?"

He sobered. "She was going to bring it, but I offered to save her the trip. And it's a good thing. If she heard you talking like that, she would not be pleased."

Adrie moaned. "I'm sorry. That wasn't nice." Her nose tickled. She yanked another tissue from the box, but she was not fast enough to catch her sneeze. "Sorry." She dabbed at her nose. "Hope you don't catch this."

"Don't worry. I have great immunity, hardly ever get sick." He held up the plastic container. "So, soup now or later?"

"Now would be nice. Thanks," she added with an apologetic half smile.

"Okay. Be right back."

She sank into her pillow and closed her eyes. Knowing someone cared enough to check on her was comforting. It was a little disconcerting that Ross was the one doing the checking, but she wasn't going to complain.

He returned a few minutes later carrying a tray with a steaming bowl of soup, some crackers, a napkin and a spoon. He certainly seemed to find his way around the kitchen easily, maybe that was because the layout of both apartments was the same.

"That looks good." She sat up slowly, but her head still pounded. Lifting her hand, she massaged her forehead.

Ross frowned. "Have you taken any medication?"

"Not since about seven this morning."

"Adrie, it's almost two o'clock." He set down the tray and reached for the grocery bag. "Here, take your pick. I stopped at the drugstore and got a few things." He set two different cold medications on the coffee table along with a box of throat lozenges, two bottles of water, a box of tissues and a women's fashion magazine.

Adrie looked up at him. "A fashion magazine?"

He shrugged. "I thought you might like some mindless reading."

"Thanks." A slight smile lifted the corners of her mouth. He seemed to know her better than she'd realized.

He reached into the bag once more. "I also brought you a few DVDs from my collection in case you're bored."

Adrie glanced at the titles, and surprise rippled through her. "You like *Casablanca* and *Out of Africa?*"

"Sure. They're classics. The photography in *Out of Africa* is amazing."

"Those are two of my favorites."

He grinned, looking pleased with himself. "Well, what do you know, that's something else we have in common."

"Did you know *Out of Africa* was filmed in Kenya?"

"I thought it might be."

Her cell phone rang. She reached for it and checked the caller ID. "Oh, it's my mom. I should take this."

"Sure. Go ahead." He walked toward the kitchen.

She watched him go, wondering what he planned to do. No time to worry about that now. Her mom usually communicated by email, so phone calls from Kenya were a rare treat. She tapped the screen and lifted the phone to her ear. "Hi, Mom."

"Hi, honey. Marian emailed and said you weren't feeling well, so I thought I'd call and check on you before I go to bed."

"Thanks. It's just a cold. I should be okay in a day or two."

"Have you been taking care of yourself? Are you eating well and getting enough sleep? Taking your vitamins?"

Adrie couldn't help smiling. "Yes, Mom, I'm being a good girl."

"Sorry, honey. I know you're an adult, but I'll always be your mother, and I'm never going to stop loving you and wanting to know how you're doing."

Her throat tightened, and unexpected tears burned in her eyes. This was silly. She'd lived half a world away from her parents for almost seven years. But hearing her mother's voice brought a fresh wave of pain to the surface.

"Thanks, Mom. I'm glad you called. Is Dad there?" The hope of talking to her father lifted her spirits. She loved him, but he wasn't very good at staying in touch. It had been at least three months since they'd spoken on the phone.

"No, he's up in Turkana teaching at a pastor's conference this week."

She tried to swallow away her disappointment. "Oh."

"He'll be back on Saturday. I'll let him know we talked."

Adrie cleared her throat. "Okay. You don't have to tell him I'm sick. I'm sure I'll be fine by then. I don't want him to worry."

"All right, dear." Her mother launched into a review of her activities for the last few weeks. Then she shifted gears to tell her about a few friends. "Remember Ann Marie Snyder? She was a year behind you at RVA."

"Sure. How is she doing?" Adrie nibbled on a cracker and stirred her soup. Fragrant steam rose and tickled her nose.

"Ann Marie married Michael Artman from your class. They came out to work in Nairobi with our mission last year, and they just had a baby girl. They named her Haley Joy. Oh, you should see her. She is just a little doll. She looks just like her mother."

"Wow, Ann Marie and Mike had a baby?" It seemed like just yesterday she and Ann Marie had run across the RVA soccer fields, hiked to the waterfalls, and spent time laughing and talking about the future. Life had moved on for her friends and family, but that didn't bother her nearly as much as realizing she was continents away and missing it all.

Memories filled her mind—her parents and younger brother, Steve; her school days at Rift Valley Academy; the beautiful dark-skinned African students from the Bible college where her father taught; the brilliant aqua Indian Ocean, colorful sunbirds, the purple jacaranda trees, the fresh scent of the rain after months of sunshine and endless red dust.

All that was familiar from her growing-up years in Kenya had been stripped away when she returned to the U.S. Her music had been the only constant, bridging her old life to the new. But even after seven years, she sometimes still felt like a disconnected stranger in her homeland.

A huge chunk of her heart remained in Kenya, and even music couldn't begin to fill the gaping hole there. A tear slipped down her cheek. She sniffed and brushed it away.

Ross walked back into the room carrying the kitchen trash can. He glanced at her, and his steps slowed. Lines of concern creased his forehead.

She looked away, snatched a tissue and wiped her nose. Her mother continued talking, telling her how happy her African friends were now that the rainy season had started and they could expect a good harvest in a few weeks.

Such simple joys in such a complicated world.

Ross quietly circled the living room, tossed two days' worth of old newspapers in the trash can. He knelt beside her and picked up the used tissues from the floor. He hesitated and their gazes met.

Adrie pulled the phone away from her ear. "You don't have to do that."

"It's okay. Enjoy your conversation." He stood and straightened the stack of magazines on the coffee table, then carried two dirty glasses and the trash can back to the kitchen. A few seconds later, he returned and stood by the end of the couch with a question in his eyes.

Adrie lifted her finger, signaling him to wait. Her conversation with her mother was winding down, and she didn't want him to leave yet.

"Thanks for calling, Mom. It means a lot." She smoothed the blanket over her legs, avoiding Ross's gaze. "I love you. Tell Dad I love him, too."

"I will, honey. Take care of yourself. Let me know how you're doing tomorrow."

"I will." Adrie said goodbye, then tapped the screen to end their conversation.

"Good call?" Ross asked, still standing by the end of the couch.

She nodded, knowing her voice would betray her if she tried to speak.

He watched her for a moment more. "Everything okay?"

She pressed her lips tightly and nodded, then quickly shook her head as tears blurred her vision. There was no sense in trying to hide her tears from him. One thing she'd learned about Ross, he was too perceptive to be fooled by her denial.

"Want to tell me about it?"

"Not sure that's a good idea."

"Why not?"

"I'll start crying if I do."

"It's okay. I'm used to tears. I have two sisters."

She blotted her eyes with her tissue. "I'll be okay. I'm just feeling a little homesick."

He sat on the love seat and settled back against the cushions, waiting for her to continue.

"Sometimes it's just really hard living halfway around the world from my family."

"I'm sure it is. Sounds like you have a good relationship with them in spite of that."

"Pretty good. We have our struggles," she said, thinking of her father's busy schedule and lack of communication. "I know they love me, and I love them. But the distance is tough, especially at times like this."

"You mean when you're sick?"

She nodded. "Or when I'm feeling stressed, or just not sure what's happening next in life. Like now." She sank back against her pillow. "I wish I could hop in the car and drive home for the weekend. Phone calls and email are a blessing, but it's not the same as having a relaxed conversation with your family. I miss that so much."

"How long since you've seen them?"

"They came out for my graduation and for my grandpa's funeral. But it's been almost two years since they were here."

"When was the last time you flew back to Kenya?"

"Too long." She swallowed. "Almost four years."

He slowly shook his head.

"I may be an American, but I spent so many years in Kenya it will always feel like home to me."

"So you not only miss your family, you miss your life there. It's part of who you are, and you're still not totally used to being so far from home."

Her breath caught in her throat. "Yes. That's exactly how I feel."

Sympathy pooled in his dark eyes. "I'm not sure how you do it—live so far away from the people who are so important to you."

She shrugged, trying to steel herself against the compassion in his voice. If she didn't, she just might break down. "Everyone has struggles they have to face," she said, forcing out the words.

He watched her, his expression insightful and caring. "True, but that doesn't mean yours aren't painful."

"Yes, some days it's still really difficult." A tremor passed through her, and she released a deep breath. Speaking those words aloud felt like opening the window and letting a fresh breeze waft through.

When was the last time she'd been so honest and opened her heart to someone like that?

The few times she'd told Adam how much she missed her family, he'd tried to change the subject. He had never been comfortable talking about emotions, and he definitely didn't know how to handle her tears.

But Ross seemed to want to understand her thoughts and feelings.

"I should get back to the store." He rose from the love

seat. "Are you going to be okay? Can I get you anything else?"

"No, I'll be fine. Thanks for the soup and for listening. Sorry I got all emotional."

"I don't mind. We all need someone to talk to sometimes." A slight grin lifted one side of his mouth. "That's what friends are for."

Though her head still ached and her nose was drippy, a smile formed on her lips. "Thanks."

"You're welcome." With one more smile over his shoulder, he headed out the door.

Chapter Ten

Ross glanced around the church foyer, chose the best background and waved Cam over. "Let's take a couple more photos by this window."

Cam shot a distracted glance down the hallway toward the room where his bride and her attendants were dressing. "What time is it?"

Ross checked his watch. "Two-fifteen."

Cam's eyes widened. "Only forty-five minutes. How are we doing? Do you have enough time to take the rest of the pictures before the ceremony?"

"Don't worry. We're right on schedule." He'd already shot a whole series of Cam with his four groomsmen and Rachel with her bridesmaids. Next he'd bring in Rachel and do the photos of Cam and Rachel together, then the whole wedding party in the sanctuary.

Ross positioned Cam to catch the best light. "Okay, turn a little to the left. Chin up. Look right here." Ross held his breath and took the shot. "Perfect."

"Can't believe we're getting married on the hottest day in September," Cam muttered and wiped his glistening forehead with the back of his hand.

Lowering his camera, Ross grinned at his friend. "Relax,

man. You're marrying the woman of your dreams today. Everything is going to be fine." He wasn't usually that straightforward with the groom when he photographed a wedding, but Cam was his good friend, so he decided to shoot straight.

"Right." Cam rubbed his hands on his black tux pants and blew out a shaky breath. "I don't know why I'm so nervous. I've been looking forward to this for months."

"Sure, but this is a big step for both of you. It makes sense you're feeling a little anxious. That'll pass."

"I just want everything to be perfect for Rachel. She deserves a great wedding."

Ross gave him a reassuring nod. "Don't worry. Everything is going to run like clockwork. She's done an amazing job with all the details."

"Yeah, she has." Cam turned and faced Ross. "Thanks for everything you're doing. We really appreciate it." He stepped forward and gave Ross a bear hug.

The camera got in the way, but Ross didn't mind. He grinned and slapped Cam on the back a couple times. "No problem. I'm glad to do it."

Cam stepped away, flexed his hands, then shook them out and paced over to the window.

Poor guy. "I know just what you need."

Cam turned, his blue eyes wide. "What?"

"A few minutes with your bride." Ross sent him a reassuring smile. "Let me go check and see if she's ready."

Cam straightened. "Right. Good idea. As soon as I see her, I'll be fine."

"Hang on. I'll be right back." Ross took off across the foyer.

If anyone deserved a second chance at happiness, it was his friend Cam. He'd lost his first wife and baby boy in a tragic auto accident almost five years ago. The weight of guilt he carried for asking his wife to drive that stormy night almost took him under. He left his high-pressure corporate job and opened a small frame shop at the Fairhaven Arts Center, hoping that would give him a new focus while he pulled his life back together. Then he met Rachel, director of North Coast Christian Youth Theater, and he found a reason to open his heart to love once more.

Ross smiled, thinking of the way that relationship had transformed Cam's life. It was nothing short of a blessing from God. Ross couldn't be happier for both of them.

Yes, Rachel deserved a great wedding day, but so did Cam. And Ross was determined to do everything he could to make it happen.

He knocked on the door of the classroom turned dressing room.

"Just a minute," a frustrated female voice called.

"Okay. It's time for some more photos as soon as Rachel's ready."

"Be out in a few," the same voice called.

The side door to the church parking lot opened. Ross glanced over his shoulder.

Adrie stepped in carrying her flute case and purse. She wore a sleeveless, rust-colored dress made of material that shimmered as it flowed over her attractive curves. Her hair was up with a few tendrils curling around her face. Around her slender neck she wore a gold beaded necklace that matched her earrings. She smiled as she walked toward him.

Ross's heartbeat picked up the pace, and his mouth went dry. "Wow, you look amazing."

Her eyes widened for a split second and her cheeks flushed. "Thanks." She shifted her flute case to the other hand. "Have you seen Rachel and Cam? How's everything going?"

"We're on schedule. They're both a little nervous, but that's normal." He pointed toward the classroom door. "The girls are in there. I'm just waiting to take Rachel to see Cam. We'll get some photos of them together, and—"

"Wait." Surprise flashed in her eyes. "He's going to see her now, before she walks down the aisle?"

Ross nodded. "They don't want to keep their guests waiting too long at the reception, so we're taking some of the photos before the ceremony."

"That's different." She glanced to the other end of the foyer where Cam waited with his groomsmen, and her expression softened. "I always like watching the groom's face when those doors open and he sees his bride for the first time." Her eyes took on a dreamy look, as though she was imagining walking toward her own groom.

No doubt she'd be a beautiful bride, so beautiful her groom would probably be stunned and speechless. He swallowed and tried to shake off that mental image. "A lot of couples do it the old-fashioned way." His voice came out low and husky.

"Well, it is their special day," she said, gazing at Cam. "They should be able to do it any way they want."

"I don't think you'll be disappointed. I bet he'll still be glowing like a lighthouse when Rachel walks down the aisle. Believe me, the guy is psyched."

Adrie laughed softly. "Okay. I won't scold them for their choice." She hesitated, glancing around. "Well, I better go. I need to run through the music once more with the pianist."

Ross reached for her arm. "Hey, why don't you stick around for a minute? Then you can watch when Cam sees Rachel for the first time."

Her face lit up, but just as quickly her expression dimmed. "No, I better not. That should be a private moment."

"It's okay. The whole wedding party will be here plus their parents."

Adrie bit her lip. "Where are they going to meet?"

He pointed to the left. "Right here in the foyer."

Her smile returned. "Okay. Thanks. I'll stay in the background."

The Sunday school room door opened, and they both turned toward it. Chandra Wetzel, Rachel's maid of honor, stepped out and motioned Ross over.

He glanced at Adrie, wishing he could stay with her, but he had a wedding to shoot. He hoped he could break away later, at the reception, and spend some more time with her. Maybe that would give him another chance to show her that he could be more than just a good friend.

Adrie smoothed her damp hand down her dress. She had changed twice before finally deciding on this outfit. She was going for a classic, understated look, since she was sitting up front while she played her flute. She didn't want to draw attention to herself or outshine the bridal party. Considering Ross's reaction, she wasn't so sure she'd made the right choice now.

Ross crossed to the foyer to answer Chandra Wetzel's summons.

The youth theater choreographer looked stunning in her knee-length, raspberry chiffon dress that showed off her great figure and toned legs. Her strawberry-blond hair was swept up with a cascade of wavy curls down the back, and over her ear she'd pinned two hot-pink orchids that matched her dress.

Chandra laid her hand on Ross's arm and leaned in close to whisper something in his ear. Ross nodded, and they shared a concerned look.

Adrie clutched the handle of her flute case and strained to hear what they were saying, but their voices were too low. Chandra was probably relaying some message from Rachel, but Adrie's stomach tensed as she watched them.

Chandra exchanged a few more words with Ross, then she leaned in and kissed his cheek.

Adrie's eyes widened. What did *that* mean? Of course they knew each other from the Arts Center where Ross used to have his photo studio and Chandra taught dance to the kids in the theater program. They also shared a mutual connection through Cam and Rachel. It made sense they would be friends. But that kiss wasn't a quick, friendly peck. It looked more like a you-are-someone-very-special kind of kiss. And Ross didn't seem the least bit surprised by it.

Her thoughts shifted back to the day she and Ross had driven up to Marys Peak. Ross had talked about how great it was when you found someone who shared common interests and experiences. Adrie thought he'd been hinting at his interest in her, but maybe he had been talking about Chandra all the time.

Why did she have such a terrible time figuring out men and relationships? How many times had she misread a man's intentions? Closing her eyes, she tried to erase the image of Chandra and Ross together, but it seemed burned on the back of her eyelids.

What difference did it make if Ross and Chandra were together? Why should that bother her? She'd told him that she didn't want anything more than friendship. What did she expect? A great guy like Ross was not going to stay unattached for long.

Suddenly, waiting around in the foyer didn't seem like such a good idea. She turned and walked toward the side door of the sanctuary.

"Adrie, wait," Ross called.

She glanced back as he approached.

"I thought you wanted to be here when Cam sees Rachel."

She shook her head. "I don't want to intrude."

Ross studied her with a quizzical look. "I'm bringing them all into the sanctuary for group photos in about five minutes. You're going to see them before the ceremony, one way or the other." He tipped his head and smiled. "Come on, it's okay." He held out his hand.

She looked down at his extended fingers and slowly reached out.

He grasped her hand firmly and his smile spread wider. Warmth and confidence flowed through their clasped hands as he led her across the foyer.

He led her to a small alcove with a padded bench. "Wait right here. I'll be back with Rachel in just a minute." He gently squeezed her fingers and winked before he let go, then turned and walked away.

Tingles traveled up her arm as she sank onto the bench. Adrie sighed and shook her head. How could holding hands with Ross for five seconds make her feel so off balance?

No, she did not want to go there right now. Closing her eyes, she focused on her music. That was her gift to Rachel and Cam. And she intended to play those pieces perfectly, setting a romantic mood for them and all who attended the ceremony. That was the least she could do for her friends, and maybe it would be enough to distract her from a certain charming photographer.

"Ladies and gentlemen, Cam and Rachel McKenna will now share their first dance as husband and wife."

Adrie clapped, then scooted her chair to the left so she had a better view. The romantic strains of "I Believe I Can Fly," played in a soft jazz style, filled the air. Cam took Rachel in his arms, and together they swirled across the dance floor.

Lilly Wong, one of Cam and Rachel's friends from the Arts Center, smiled at Adrie from across the table. "They look so happy."

"Yes, they seem lost in their own world." Adrie sat back and released a soft sigh. Wouldn't it be wonderful to find someone who loved her like that?

Melanie Howard, another Arts Center friend, placed her hot-pink cloth napkin on the table. "I can't believe the way they transformed this room. It looks totally different than the last time I was here."

Adrie glanced around. The second-floor Dome Room of the Bellingham Cruise Terminal was an amazing place for a reception. At one end of the large room, floor-to-ceiling windows in a half-circle created a glass dome overlooking Bellingham Bay. Ribbon streamers in hot-pink, tangerine and lime-green decorated the entrance, and tiny white lights hung from the ceiling along the edge of the dome. Beautiful floral arrangements of white orchids, orange roses and hot-pink Gerber daisies brightened each table. The little gold votive candleholders Adrie had helped Rachel decorate sat in front of each place as a gift for the guests to take home.

Everything was perfect, except she was seated at a table of other single friends who were attending without a date. She glanced around the room and spotted Ross on the far side of the dance floor. He had taken off his black suit jacket and rolled up the sleeves of his white dress shirt. Lifting his camera, he focused on Cam and Rachel and shot a series of photos from a discreet distance as they continued their dance.

He had been busy since he arrived and had only taken one short break to grab a few bites of salad and a roll. The rest of his dinner remained untouched on his plate. Adrie had no idea when he'd return and finish his meal.

The sun dipped lower in the western sky, and the view changed to vibrant shades of pink, magenta and gold—a perfect reflection of the wedding colors. Lights flickered from the boats in the bay.

The beat of the music sped up, and several other couples joined Cam and Rachel on the dance floor. Adrie laid her knife and fork across her plate and pushed it forward. The food was delicious, but she'd been full after the appetizers and salad. She'd hardly touched the prime rib, roasted potatoes and vegetables.

"Well, I'm ready to dance," Lilly said. "Anyone else want to join me?"

Steve Jackson, owner of Cakewalk bakery and the designer of Cam and Rachel's wedding cake, grabbed another roll from the basket and stuffed half in his mouth while he silently shook his head.

Ryan Ortman, local EMT and fireman, shifted in his seat and exchanged a nervous glance with Steve. "I'm not much of a dancer."

Melanie pursed her lips, looking perturbed, and pushed back from the table. "Who needs men to have a good time? Let's get a line dance started." Melanie lifted her chin and sauntered off toward the DJ.

Lilly sent them an apologetic smile, then followed Melanie toward the dance floor.

Noelle Jackson, Steve's sister, grinned at Adrie. "Line dancing sounds fun. You want to give it a try?"

"Sure." Adrie hopped up and followed the petite blonde to the dance floor where a whole group of young women had gathered, waiting for the next song.

Melanie and Lilly walked toward the group with Chandra Wetzel in tow.

Chandra stepped out front and held up her hands. In choreographer mode, she walked them through the dance twice, counting out the steps and explaining the moves as she went along. Then she signaled the DJ to start the music.

Adrie caught on quickly, and soon she was following the fun steps with ease. Cam, Rachel and the rest of the wedding party joined in. The dance floor filled as young and old alike joined in, laughing and dancing to the lively country tune.

When the song ended, Adrie clapped along with everyone else. The gentle strains of a slow, romantic song came on next. She drifted to the edge of the dance floor to catch her breath.

Just as she was about to head back to her seat, someone tapped her on the shoulder.

"Would you like to dance?"

Her heart leaped as she turned around. She blinked and looked up at Ross.

He smiled, golden lights flickering in his dark brown eyes. "Come on. It will be fun."

Adrie swallowed. "Okay, but I'm not a very good dancer." She took a tentative step forward and placed her left hand in his right, suddenly feeling shy.

"That's not true. I've been watching you. You're a great dancer." He placed his left hand on her upper back, drawing her closer. The warmth from his hand flooded through her.

Her face flushed. "Well, line dancing is different than… this." She placed her right hand on his shoulder. Beneath the smooth fabric of his dress shirt, she could feel the solid strength of his upper arm and shoulder. She pressed her lips together and tried to gather her wits, but her heart hammered so hard she could barely think.

"Ready?"

She nodded, and he guided her into the dance, his steps smooth and confident as he led her around the floor in perfect time to the music.

She tried to match his movements, but her efforts felt stiff and hesitant compared to his. That didn't seem to bother him. He continued to guide her through each turn with ease. Ballroom dancing was obviously another of his hidden talents. He must have taken dance classes or had private lessons. A sudden thought jolted through her. Had Chandra taught him to dance?

She stiffened and lost count of the steps. Biting her lip, she tried to regain her focus, but she misjudged his next move and stepped on his foot. "Oh, no." She winced and pulled away. "I'm sorry."

"Relax." He pulled her closer again. "Don't worry about it."

"But your toes..."

"I'm fine."

She groaned inwardly at her clumsiness. She was not a skilled dancer like Chandra Wetzel. The flirty, outgoing choreographer was probably a lot more fun on the dance floor and everywhere else. "Sorry. I haven't done much dancing," Adrie murmured.

He chuckled. "No more apologies. You're doing fine. Just think of it like playing a piece of music."

"What do you mean?"

He waited until she lifted her eyes to meet his. "With a little practice, it gets easier and easier, until you don't even have to think about it anymore. It just flows, and you make beautiful music." The intimate look in his eyes suggested he was talking about more than just the dance.

She willed herself to relax in his arms and follow his lead. The music built and soared. The next steps came easier, and soon she found herself floating along, smiling up at him.

"There you go." He nodded, and sent her a warm, encouraging smile.

Being in his arms and looking up into his eyes felt so right. They glided around the floor, her heart growing lighter with each step.

Suddenly, his expression changed slightly. The pressure of his hand on her back increased, and he held her more tightly.

"Ross?" a feminine voice behind Adrie broke through the music.

He slowed and turned slightly, but he didn't let go. "Yes?"

Chandra Wetzel came into view. Her gaze darted from Adrie to Ross. "Sorry to interrupt, but they're getting ready to cut the cake. I'm sure Rachel and Cam will want those pictures."

He nodded slightly to Chandra, then focused on Adrie, regret in his eyes. "I'm sorry," he murmured, gently releasing her. "Maybe we can finish our dance later."

"It's okay." She forced a smile and stepped back.

Chandra tucked her hand into the crook of his arm and guided him back toward the head table.

Adrie frowned slightly as her gaze followed them. Rachel and Cam were still seated, and there was no activity near the cake table.

"Wow, looks like she just snatched Ross right out of your arms," Noelle said, appearing at her side. "What's going on?"

"I guess it's time to cut the cake."

Noelle cocked her head as she watched them. "Already?"

"That's what Chandra said."

"Couldn't she have waited until the song ended? What's the big rush?"

Adrie sighed and shook her head. "I suppose she was just trying to be sure he doesn't miss those photos."

"Well, I guess it's a good thing she gave us a heads-up." Noelle lifted her small digital camera. "I promised Steve I'd take some photos of them cutting the cake. If they come out okay, he wants to put them on the bakery website."

"Sounds like a good idea." Adrie had stopped by the cake table earlier to see the gorgeous, four-tiered, hexagonal cake with pink, orange and green flowers between each tier. "What kind of cake is it?"

"One layer is spicy carrot with lots of raisins and walnuts. The others are bittersweet chocolate, cherry and orange. And each slice will be served with cantaloupe or raspberry sorbet."

"Wow, that sounds delicious."

Noelle grinned. "I'm sure you won't be disappointed."

Adrie's smile faded as they walked across the room. She might not be disappointed by the cake, but she couldn't help feeling let down by missing the last half of the dance with Ross.

Chapter Eleven

Adrie flipped off the kitchen light and walked into her living room. She usually loved these quiet Sunday evenings. She could relax, plan for the next week and practice her flute. But tonight the silence seemed to press in around her, leaving her feeling anxious and restless.

She'd taken her flute out an hour ago but then wandered back into the kitchen, alphabetized her spices, straightened all the items in her pantry and rearranged her utensil drawer.

Why couldn't she settle down and focus on her music?

She strode over to the end table and picked up her flute. As she raised it to her lips, memories from Cam and Rachel's wedding came rushing back. She'd loved playing for them. After the ceremony, Rachel had thanked her with tears in her eyes.

Everything about the wedding had been perfect—the flowers, the dresses, the ceremony, the reception. But the highlight for Adrie had been dancing with Ross. Even now, the memory of his warm hand on her back as he guided her through each turn made her stomach flutter. In those few moments he'd made her feel so special.

She squeezed her eyes shut. What was she doing? This was crazy. She wouldn't deny she was attracted to Ross, but they were friends. Period. And that was as far as she intended to let things go. How many times would she have to tell herself that before her heart got the message?

She adjusted her fingers and focused on the sheet music. She ought to be thinking about launching her music career, not some fantasy romance that was never going to happen.

A knock sounded at her apartment door. She set her flute aside and answered the door.

Ross stood in the hallway, carrying his laptop case and a large paper bag with *A.W. Asian Bistro* printed on the side. A spicy scent rose from the bag and tickled her nose.

"I brought home some Thai food, and I thought you might be hungry."

She stared at him for a second. This was so strange. She had just been telling herself to stop thinking about him, and here he was, standing in her doorway.

He tipped his head and smiled. "So…can I come in?"

"Oh, sure." She stood back so he could pass through. It was okay. They were friends, and friends stopped in to see each other unannounced. There was nothing wrong with that.

"I loaded all the wedding photos on my computer this afternoon. I thought you might like to see them."

"Even before you show Cam and Rachel?"

"I'm sure they won't care, since they're off enjoying their honeymoon." He grinned and winked at her.

"Right." Her cheeks flushed.

"I want to take out the duds before I show them. But I didn't think you'd mind seeing the first round."

Her heart warmed at his words. "I'd love to see them." She scooted aside the candle and magazines on the coffee table and sat down next to him on the couch. He opened the computer and clicked through to the photo program.

"You can probably see them better if you hold the computer on your lap." He handed it to her and scooted closer until his arm and shoulder touched hers.

A delightful shiver traveled up her arm, and she silently scolded herself. Focusing on the screen, she looked through the first few photos. The composition and angle made each shot unique, and the background and lighting added texture and contrast "Wow, they're beautiful, Ross."

"I hope they like them."

"I'm sure they will." She took a closer look at the series he'd taken in the foyer before the ceremony when Cam saw Rachel for the first time. "Oh, I love this one." Ross had captured that priceless look of wonder and intimacy in Cam's eyes as well as the love in Rachel's expression.

"Yeah, that's one of my favorites."

"These are amazing." She turned to him. "You're not just a photographer, you're an artist."

"Thanks." He grinned, a teasing light in his eyes. "Hope you'll recommend me to all your friends."

"If I do, you might not want to work at the bookstore anymore." She'd worried about that since the day they'd hired him, but as soon as the words left her mouth, she regretted them.

All the humor drained from his expression. "I won't walk out on you, Adrie. I promise."

"But this is what you really want." She gestured toward the computer. "Right?"

He frowned slightly. "Yes, eventually. But I'm content doing it part-time for now."

She slowly shook her head. "I don't want to keep you from doing what you love."

"You're not." He reached for her hand.

She leaned forward, sliding her hand away from his, and placed the open laptop on the coffee table. Her throat tightened and burned.

He watched her closely. "Adrie, what's wrong?"

She shrugged, her thoughts a jumbled mess. "We're both waiting for something important to change in our lives."

He nodded. "Waiting can be tough. But if we trust God, when the time is right, He'll do what's best for us."

His faith-filled words cut her to the heart. When was the last time she'd prayed about her future and the decisions she needed to make?

It had been weeks since she'd taken time in the morning to read her Bible and talk to the Lord. She had been so sure she was headed in the right direction that she hadn't even bothered to ask Him to confirm her plans. She'd just assumed all her training and preparation made a professional music career the right path. But what if she was wrong? What if that was not what God wanted for her? She shook her head, blinking back her tears.

"Hey, don't worry. Everything is going to work out. When I heard you play at the wedding, I was blown away. You're the one who has a gift. And one of these days, God's going to open the door, and you'll hear about a position that's just right for you."

She swallowed hard. "I heard about one today."

He blinked. "You did?"

She nodded. "My teacher from Morrowstone called this afternoon. She has connections at the Minnesota Philharmonic in Minneapolis. Their second flutist is having a baby and giving up her spot. They'll probably post the position online some time this week. She wants me to apply."

"Wow. Minneapolis."

Her shoulders sagged. "Yeah, that's what I said."

"But it's what you want, right?"

Adrie pressed her lips together and nodded. If that was true, then why did she feel so torn? Her gaze blurred and she blinked back hot tears. "I guess I'm just feeling a little overwhelmed by the thought of moving so far away."

"That makes sense. I mean, you're not just talking about going to Seattle or Vancouver… This is halfway across the country."

She pushed up from the couch. "Well, I shouldn't worry. A lot of people will want that spot. I might not even get to audition."

"How do they decide?"

"Each orchestra is a little different, but usually you send in a résumé and sometimes a CD. If they like those, they ask you to come to a preliminary audition. If you make that cut, then there's a final audition."

He blew out a deep breath. "Does the Minneapolis group want you to send a CD?"

"I'm not sure. Lucia said she'd try to find out more details, but she wants me to update my résumé and get a CD ready."

He nodded. "I'm sure if they hear you play, you'll get the job. When I heard you yesterday…wow, I couldn't take a single photo during that song."

Her throat tightened again, and a tear slipped down her cheek. How could he be so sweet to her, when she'd continually pushed him away?

"Hey, I'm not trying to make you cry. Come here." He opened his arms, and she fell into his hug.

"I don't know why I'm being such a baby." She sniffed and rested her head against his shoulder.

"This could be a huge change in your life. It's worthy of a few tears."

"Thanks, Ross."

"For?"

"Being such a great friend."

She felt him tense for a moment. Then he relaxed as he gently rubbed her back. "No problem. That's what I'm here for."

* * *

Ross turned the key and cranked his car engine for the third time. *Please, God, let it start.* The futile whirring sound filled the air, mocking him. He lifted his eyes. "What am I supposed to do now?"

With a weary shake of his head, he climbed out and popped the hood. Was it the battery? He squinted and leaned in closer, but he had no idea what he was looking for. His automotive skills ranked right up there with his cooking abilities.

Adrie drove into the bookstore's parking lot and waved to him.

He lifted his hand and forced a half smile. Adrie had asked for the morning off so she could record the CD she planned to send to the Minnesota Philharmonic. A painful, hollow feeling hit his stomach, and it had nothing to do with skipping lunch.

Adrie parked next to Ross and climbed out. "Having car trouble?"

He glared at the lifeless engine. "Yeah. It won't start."

Adrie stepped up next to him. "Wish I could help, but my skills are limited to adding fluids and checking tire pressure. And that's a stretch for me."

The same was true for him, but he hated to admit it. Instead, he reached in and wiggled a couple hoses and tapped on the battery cables. A lot of good that did. "Guess I'll have to call a tow truck and have them take it to a garage."

Clamping his jaw, he slammed the hood closed. Where would he come up with the money to pay for towing and car repairs? His budget was still strained from being out of work for two months.

His budget woes and the bookstore's were frighteningly similar. This morning Marian had called him in the office and showed him the final September sales figures, and warned him if their holiday sales weren't spectacular, the store might have to close in January. Then Adrie had left to record her CD, reminding him if he didn't win her heart soon, she would be playing her flute in Minneapolis while he ran the bookstore in Fairhaven—if there still was a bookstore to run. And now his car was on the blink!

Adrie laid her hand on his arm. "Sorry about your car. Were you on your way somewhere?"

The warmth of her hand spread through him, calming his churning thoughts. "I was going to the bank to make the deposit." He patted the envelope in his jacket pocket. "Then I was going to stop by Cam's to take in the mail and check on the house." His friends weren't due home from their Hawaiian honeymoon for another ten days.

She looked up at him with a sympathetic gaze. "I could give you a ride. Nana's not expecting me until one." She tipped her head and smiled. "And there's something I want to talk to you about."

His ears perked up. If she wanted to talk, he was eager to listen. "Thanks. That would be great."

"What about calling the tow truck?"

"I can take care of that when we get back." Ross walked around to the passenger side and climbed in. This was the first time he'd been in Adrie's car. Her dashboard was dust-free and the front window clean and clear. All her CDs were neatly lined up across the inside of her sun visor. He smiled. No surprises there. Her car matched her personality—neat and orderly, with everything in its place.

She slid behind the wheel and reached into her purse. "When I was at the university, I saw this brochure and thought of you." She handed it to him with a shy smile. "The Washington Trails Association is sponsoring a photo contest." She hesitated a second then added, "Maybe you could enter."

He scanned the headlines and read a few details. "Wow, this looks great." But knowing Adrie had been thinking about him meant even more. A smile tugged at the corners of his mouth. Maybe this wouldn't turn out to be such a terrible day after all.

Adrie pulled out of the parking lot. "The winning photos will be published in the *Washington Trails* magazine next year, and they're offering prizes to all the finalists."

Ross nodded, thinking through some of the photos he'd taken on a recent hike to Picture Lake near Mount Shuksan. The bright blue sky and snowcapped mountain were a great contrast to the fall colors in the bushes and trees surrounding the lake.

"You can only enter five photos, so maybe you should check out last year's winners online. That might give you an idea of what they're looking for."

"Good idea." He glanced at her again, his spirits rising. She'd not only thought of him when she saw the brochure, she'd read the details and come up with suggestions on how to choose the best entries.

That was a good sign, a very good sign.

Chapter Twelve

Adrie tiptoed down the hall and stopped in front of Ross's apartment door. She lifted her hand, then stopped and glanced at her watch. Would he think she was crazy for coming over so early? Probably, but for her grandmother's sake, she would risk it.

She rapped lightly on his door while her stomach tingled with nervous energy. Why was she worried? She and Ross were friends, and friends sometimes did goofy, spontaneous things like this. She knocked again, louder this time.

Muffled footsteps crossed his apartment, and the door creaked open.

Ross blinked and looked out at her. He wore navy sweatpants, a wrinkled gray T-shirt and his hair was mussed.

"Sorry, did I wake you?"

"No, I was just getting up. Is everything okay?"

"Yeah, everything's fine." She shifted her weight to the other foot. "I just…um…wondered if you'd like to go clam digging with me."

"Clam digging?" He squinted at her. "You mean like down at the beach, right now?"

She nodded. "I know it sounds crazy, but today is Grandpa Bill's birthday, and that's going to be hard for

Nana. She needs something else to focus on, and she loves clam chowder, but she hasn't made any since my grandpa died, because that was his favorite, and we used to be the ones to dig the clams for her." She was babbling, but she couldn't help it. Seeing him standing there so early in the morning was making her nervous. She swallowed. "So I thought if we brought her a big batch of fresh clams it might help."

He glanced toward the hallway window. "You know it's still dark outside, right?"

"The best low tide this week is in forty-five minutes. The sun will be up by then."

He rubbed his bristly chin. "But we have to open the store at ten."

"I'm sure we can dig our limit and be back by then."

He braced his hand against the doorframe. "So…where are we going to dig these clams?"

Her heart lifted, like a helium balloon taking flight. "Grandpa and I always went to Larrabee State Park. It's just a few miles south down Chuckanut Drive." She glanced at his clothing again. "Have you ever been clam digging before?"

"No, but it sounds fun." He cocked his head and sent her a teasing grin. "Especially if you're going to teach me."

Her face flamed. She pushed her hair over her shoulder, trying to pretend his smile didn't have any effect on her. "You'll probably get wet and sandy, so keep that in mind when you get dressed." She pointed at his bare feet. "You can wear Grandpa's rubber boots if you want. They go all the way up to your knees."

"Is that what you're wearing?" He looked her over, his grin still tilted at a teasing slant.

She glanced down at her jeans and turtleneck sweater. "Yes, plus my boots."

He chuckled. "Can't wait to see those."

"They definitely make the outfit."

"Okay. Give me five minutes." He winked at her and pulled the door closed.

Mercy! She turned away and fanned her face. How could a little wink and a few teasing phrases affect her so?

Thirty minutes later Ross sat in the passenger seat of Adrie's car as they drove down Chuckanut Drive in the misty predawn light. The sun probably wouldn't rise over the top of the mountains for another thirty minutes, but the sky over the rippling bay had lightened from soft gray to pale blue. By the time the sun finally appeared, they'd be down on the beach, digging for buried treasure.

He smiled and took a sip of coffee, still trying to shake off his surprise at the morning's events.

Adrie definitely seemed to be softening toward him. Ever since the wedding she'd been reaching out in different ways—bringing him the photo contest brochure and encouraging him to enter, offering him a ride to worship practice since his car was at the shop, dropping off a plate of home-made cookies and now, inviting him along on this early morning trip to the beach.

Cam said she'd let him know when she was ready to be more than friends. Maybe this was what he was talking about.

He hadn't dated much in the last couple years, but he knew what he was looking for, and the more he got to know Adrie, the more he felt sure she might be the one. Not only was she smart, caring and talented, she was also focused and determined to achieve her goals. That spoke of an inner strength that seemed to come from her faith and upbringing. Most of the women he'd met in the past seemed shallow and pale compared to Adrie.

He glanced over at her, studying her attractive profile— her amazing blue eyes, the gentle slope of her nose. But her beauty was not just on the surface. It flowed out from her heart. It was evident in her love for her grandmother and her friends, and each person who came in the bookstore.

She looked his way and smiled. "What?"

"Nothing." He lifted his cup and took another sip. Good thing they'd stopped for coffee before they left Fairhaven. It gave him something to focus on so he didn't stare at her the whole time they were driving.

He ran his hand over his rough chin. Too bad she hadn't given him time to shower or shave. At least he'd combed his hair and brushed his teeth, just in case. He grinned again. If things went as he hoped, maybe he'd catch more than just a few clams this morning.

Something was going on with Ross. Adrie glanced at him again, then quickly pulled her focus back to the curving road. Why did he keep smiling at her like that? Crazy guy—she could hardly resist the urge to reach over and poke his arm and tell him to stop.

And how come he looked so good when she'd only given him five minutes to get ready? She quickly banished that thought. But the more time they spent together, the harder it became to resist her attraction to him. The differences she originally thought would make them an unlikely match now seemed to make him interesting and even endearing.

If only they'd met when she was settled in her new job and ready to invest in a relationship. But her course was set to sail away from Fairhaven, and his was firmly anchored here. And leaving Fairhaven might be happening sooner rather than later.

She shot him a quick sideways glance. "I got a call from the people in Minneapolis last night."

He looked down at his coffee cup. "What did they say?"

"They wanted to know more about my Morrowstone fellowship."

He looked up.

"That's a summer music program for teens and college students. I was involved for five years."

He took a sip of his coffee, looking somber.

"They also asked about my early music training. I guess they thought since I was raised in Kenya I wouldn't have access to lessons. I told them I attended Rift Valley Academy since I was eleven and studied flute there."

"Sounds like they're serious."

"Maybe. I'll have to wait and see." She gripped the steering wheel as her mental wrestling match over her future surfaced again. An opportunity with a well-established orchestra like the Minnesota Philharmonic didn't come up often. It was the only open position she'd found in the past few months. She'd heard Minneapolis was a beautiful city, but it would be nothing like Fairhaven…and it was so far away.

"Did they tell you anything else?"

"The preliminary audition is November 3, so I should find out soon if they want me to come."

He stared out the front window, his mouth set in a grim line.

Time to change the subject. She didn't want to put a damper on their day. "Any news when you might get your car back?"

"They had to order a part—a very expensive part, I might add." He grimaced.

"It was nice Cam let you borrow his SUV," she added, hoping to shift his focus again to something more positive.

"Yeah, I can't afford to be without a car right now. I've got a couple of photo jobs this weekend. And I need that money to cover the car repair bill."

She wished she could reach over and squeeze his hand, but that would probably send the wrong message. "If you need an advance on your paycheck, I'm sure we could work that out."

A muscle in his jaw flickered. "No thanks. I just need to keep on praying for extra jobs and watch my expenses."

She sent him a sympathetic glance.

"Don't worry. I'll figure it out. I'm a very resourceful guy." One side of his mouth lifted in a slight smile, but it didn't quite reach his eyes.

The sign for Larrabee State Park came into view. She turned off and followed the road to the beach parking lot. They climbed out and walked around back to the trunk. Adrie reached in for the mesh bag and clipped it to her belt.

Ross fingered the bag and gave it a playful tug, pulling her toward him. "What's this for?"

She laughed and tugged it away from him. "It holds all the clams we're going to dig." She passed him the clam gun. "Here you go."

He grabbed the handle and looked into the long hollow tube. "And what am I supposed to do with this?"

She grinned. "It's a clam gun."

"Oh, well, that makes sense." He raised it to his shoulder and aimed toward the beach. "Bang! There, that ought to get us a good batch of clams."

She chuckled and shook her head. "That's not exactly how you use it."

"Okay. Not a problem. I'm sure you'll give me a lesson."

"Of course." She sat on the back fender, pulled off her shoes, and stepped into her black rubber boots with pink and red polka dots.

Ross's eyes widened. "Wow, those sure make a fashion statement."

"A girl has to look her best, even while digging clams." She smiled up at him, then hopped up and slammed the trunk. "Ready to go?"

He lifted his hand in the direction of the beach. "Lead the way."

Toting their shovels and clam gun, they crossed the parking lot and took the trail to the beach. Soon they were strolling down the shoreline side by side.

"Hello, anybody home down there?" Ross called in a playful voice as he tapped his shovel handle on the sand. "You sure this is how it's done?"

She chuckled. "That's how grandpa did it. He said the tapping makes them start digging, and then you can see a little indention." She continued walking and tapping, her eyes glued to the sand. She gasped. "Like that!"

"What do we do now?"

"We dig, quick and careful." She plunged her shovel into the muddy sand a few inches away from the indention. Salt water seeped back in and quickly filled the hole. They scooped out several more shovelfuls, then Adrie knelt and reached into the frigid, soupy puddle.

Ross squatted next to her. "I can't believe you're sticking your hand in that muck."

She laughed. "How else am I going to get him out?" Her fingers tingled from the cold as she cautiously felt around the hole. "You have to be careful, or you'll cut your hand on their shell."

He leaned closer, his expression serious.

"There it is." She gripped the clam and pulled it to the surface.

"Wow, that's a big one." A delighted grin filled his face. "Good job."

"Thanks." She walked down to the water, then bent to rinse the clam and her hands in the next little wave.

Ross followed. "You know, you're pretty amazing."

She looked up at him. "Because I know how to dig clams?" She held out the clean shell for his inspection.

"That is a special skill." He took the clam and slipped it into the net bag, then reached for her hand.

His warm grasp engulfed her wet, chilly fingers, and all her senses came alive.

He gently rubbed her palm with his thumb. "It's hard to believe a woman who plays the flute so beautifully would dig through a muddy hole like that for her grandma's sake." A look of tenderness filled his eyes. "You are one special lady, Adrie Chandler." His gaze traveled over her face and finally settled on her mouth.

She looked up at him, her heart opening like a blossom on a warm summer day. His dark eyes mesmerized her, and all the reasons she should not kiss him faded from her mind. He leaned down and gently brushed his lips across hers. She let her eyes drift closed and lost herself in his earnest, searching kiss.

He caressed her cheek and deepened the kiss, and her painful longing to be loved and cherished seemed to ease. Lost in the moment, she melted against him.

A wave splashed on their feet, surprising them both and breaking the romantic spell. Adrie stepped back, her lips burning.

He chuckled softly. "Getting up early to go clam digging has just become my favorite way to start the day."

Her heart pounded out an erratic rhythm. How could she have kissed Ross? What was she thinking? Maybe that was the problem—she wasn't thinking at all. She'd just followed her feelings not considering where they would lead.

His grin melted away. "What's wrong?"

"I'm sorry... I shouldn't have... I didn't mean..."

His eyes widened. "Oh, no, are you one of those girls who doesn't believe in kissing until the wedding?"

"No, it's not that."

Confusion clouded his eyes. "Well, what is it?"

"Kissing is for couples who are in a serious relationship, but…we're not."

He stared at her for a second, then walked a few steps away. "You beat all, Adrie. You know that? You really do."

Her heart clenched. "I'm sorry, Ross. I just—"

He turned and held up his hand. "Don't say it. And don't tell me you didn't feel anything. You kissed me back."

Her face flamed. "Okay. I admit I'm attracted to you, but it takes more than emotion and chemistry to build a lasting relationship."

"Of course it does. But it starts with attraction, and there's nothing wrong with that."

She chewed her lower lip as painful memories rose to taunt her. She'd followed her attraction to Adam, and look where that had taken her—straight into the worst betrayal of her life. She could not survive another heartbreak like that.

But Ross was different than Adam, wasn't he?

"Adrie, listen to me. I'm not playing games. I care about you. I think we could have the kind of relationship we're both looking for. But we'll never know unless you give us a chance."

She plunged her trembling hands in her jacket pockets. "I don't know, Ross."

He stepped toward her. "I'm not asking you to make up your mind right now." He reached out and gently ran his hand down the side of her cheek. "Just say you'll think about it."

His touch spread a comforting wave of warmth through her. She leaned into his hand and looked up into his eyes. "I don't want to hurt you."

"You'll only hurt me if you say no now." His sincere, steady expression pushed away her last excuse.

"Okay, but I can't make any promises."

"That's enough for me." He leaned down and kissed her cheek.

A small flicker of hope burned in her heart, but as she tried to imagine combining her dreams for the future and a relationship with Ross, the flame wavered and died.

Chapter Thirteen

Ross trudged across the bookstore, his heart sore from the beating it had taken at the beach that morning. But he had no one to blame but himself. He'd made a mess of things by kissing Adrie. Why hadn't he prayed and waited for God's direction instead of pushing ahead with his own plans?

Adrie had barely spoken to him on their ride back to town. When they had arrived at the bookstore, she had dropped him off, telling him to open the store without her. She had planned to drive to her grandmother's to drop off the clams and wouldn't be in until that afternoon.

He released a heavy sigh and unlocked the front door. As he flipped the sign to OPEN he glanced outside.

George Bradford crossed the street headed toward the bookstore.

Ross held open the door. "Morning, George."

"Hey there, my friend. How are you this fine morning?"

Ross shrugged. "I've been better. That's for sure."

"How could your day turn sour so early? It's barely ten o'clock."

"I've been up since six. Adrie and I went clam digging."

George grinned. "So…things are progressing?"

Heat climbed up Ross's neck. How had George figured

out he was interested in Adrie? Was he that obvious? There was no use pretending it wasn't true. He could use the input of another man. "I thought I was making some headway until I got my signals crossed and kissed her."

George frowned. "She wasn't happy about that?"

"That's what's confusing. While I was kissing her, she seemed to like it, but afterward she was pretty upset."

"Oh, I see." George nodded and narrowed his eyes.

"Hey, if you've got a clue what's going on, I'd sure like to know." He ran his hand through his hair. "The girl is driving me crazy."

George chuckled. "Sorry, I shouldn't be laughing at your misery. But I remember my wife reacting much the same way after our first kiss."

"Really? How did you work things out?"

"It took a few months, but she came around when she saw how much I loved her."

"What did you do to convince her?"

George's gaze drifted toward the window. "I used to pick her up every night after work so she wouldn't have to ride the bus home. Then I taught her how to drive using my brand-new VW Bug."

Ross grinned. "Wow, that's love."

George shrugged. "I shoveled her walk when it snowed, and I tutored her younger brother in math. I also paid some of her mother's medical bills. But most important, I never kissed her again until she asked me to."

Ross nodded slowly. George's advice sounded awfully familiar. Hadn't Cam told him to be a committed friend, win her heart through caring actions and wait for God's direction before he tried to move their friendship to the next level? Maybe God wanted to make sure he got the message. "Thanks, George."

George gave Ross's shoulder a firm pat. "Glad to encourage a fellow traveler on the road to romance."

"Would you like a cup of coffee?" Ross motioned toward the café. "Marian won't be in until she's done cleaning that batch of clams."

"Thanks. Coffee sounds great." George followed Ross toward the café. "Marian and I have a lunch date later, but I actually came by to talk to you about a photo job."

Ross straightened. "What do you have in mind?"

"Next Friday afternoon we've got a dozen foster kids coming to the studio with the Heart Gallery Project. Have you heard of it?"

Ross filled the coffeepot with water and flipped the switch. "I read about it in a magazine a while back, but refresh my memory."

"Photographers take portraits of foster kids who are available for adoption. The photos are posted online and shown at adoption events. A lot of kids find families that way."

"Sounds like a great idea."

George nodded. "Ray signed up a few months ago, before his health issues came up. The local project director set it up for next week. I'd fill in for him, but I promised my grandson I'd come down to Seattle on Friday to see him play football.

"So, Ray and I wondered if you could take the photos for us." George leaned against the counter. "All the photographers do it on a volunteer basis, so there's no pay, but we'll take care of developing the prints."

Ross liked the idea of using his skills to help people, especially foster kids who needed a family, but could he take more time off from the bookstore? Marian or Adrie would probably cover for him, especially when they heard the reason. "Sure, I'd be glad to do it."

George gave him a few more details. Ross jotted them down on a notepad while the coffee finished dripping. Ross poured a cup and held it out to George. "I'll run the date by

Marian, but she's been great about giving me time off when I need it."

"Thanks, Ross." George accepted the coffee. "Let me know when you get the final okay."

Ross poured himself a cup of coffee and stared down at the dark brew. George's earlier comments circled back through his mind. "Tell me about your wife."

A bittersweet emotion filled George's eyes. "Evelyn and I were married for thirty-nine years. We have two sons and a daughter and four grandkids. She passed away eight years ago from breast cancer."

Ross clenched his jaw. "I'm sorry, George."

"Thanks." George opened a pack of sugar and added it to his coffee. "We had a wonderful life together. I have many happy memories, but I still miss her."

"I'm sure you do." Ross added cream to his coffee. "Losing your wife like that must help you understand what it's been like for Marian."

"Each person's journey through grief is different, but yes, my loss gives me compassion for Marian and anyone who's lost a spouse." George sat down. "It's painful to say good-bye to someone you love, someone who shared so much of your life. But as time passes, the pain recedes some, and the lessons you've learned help you look ahead."

"What kind of lessons?" Ross asked, joining him at the table.

"Missing my wife has helped me understand the value of companionship. Sharing your life with someone you love makes the journey so much more enjoyable."

Ross nodded, thinking of Adrie and how much he looked forward to seeing her. His feelings for her were growing stronger every day even though she regretted their kiss.

"When you find that someone special, the one you love, you should do whatever it takes to win her heart." He lifted his mug toward Ross and smiled. "But I don't have to tell you that."

"Right." Ross nodded and tried to look confident, but he couldn't fool his aching heart. Confidence was the last thing he felt at the moment.

He had found someone special, someone he could love, but he had no idea if he would ever win her heart.

Chapter Fourteen

Adrie stacked three more boxes of Christmas cards on the overflowing top shelf. "It doesn't seem right that we're putting these out before the end of October."

Nana adjusted the sign attached to the display. "I know, but once we turn our calendars to November, the race toward Christmas is on."

"That's true." It also meant the first-round auditions in Minneapolis were only a week away, and she still hadn't heard if she would be going. A crazy mixture of hope and defeat wrestled in her heart.

Worry lines creased her grandmother's forehead. "And these next two months will determine our future. We need to bring in every customer we can."

Adrie scolded herself for being so self-centered when her grandmother's business was on the line. She slipped her arm around her grandma's shoulder. "Don't worry, Nana. I'm sure our Christmas sales will pull us out of this slump."

"I hope so, dear." Nana's expression eased as she glanced around the store. "Everything looks lovely. Now all we need are more shoppers."

"They'll come." Adrie leaned over and kissed her grandmother's cheek.

"Yes, we just have to keep praying and believing."

Adrie turned and surveyed the large oval table, holding a display of holiday books and gifts. "Do you think we should move the table to the left a few feet so it's not crowding the Bible section?"

Her grandmother nodded. "People will linger if they have some room to breathe. Let's do it." She stepped toward the table.

"No, Nana, it's too heavy for you. Ross will help me." She glanced over her shoulder, but she didn't see him.

"He's in the office working on the deposit."

"I'll ask him to give me a hand."

Every day Ross took over more of her responsibilities. Most of them seemed to come easily to him, but he was still learning the financial side of the business. "Maybe I'll go see if he needs any help."

"Good idea." Nana beamed. "Ross is doing wonderfully, but every man needs a little encouragement now and then." A hopeful light glowed in Nana's eyes.

Adrie turned away, pretending she didn't understand her grandma's not-so-subtle message. Nana obviously hadn't given up her matchmaking hopes for Ross and Adrie.

Ross glared at the piles of cash and checks on the desk. Why couldn't he get these numbers to match up? It didn't make sense. This was his third time counting the one hundred dollars in change for the cash drawer and adding up all the checks and bills. But he was still forty dollars short. How could money just disappear like that? Had he given out the wrong change or dropped it on the floor?

He rolled back the chair and scanned the rug under the desk. Nothing. Not a dollar, a dime or even a penny.

He shot a quick glance at the clock and shook his head. He did not have time for this. A whole list of errands needed to be taken care of before five.

He considered asking Adrie for help, but that would mean admitting he couldn't handle the deposit on his own. What would she think of him if he told her that he'd never been good with numbers?

That had been unthinkable for his CPA father. *No son of mine should be getting Cs in algebra. How are you ever going to get ahead in life if you don't pull up your grades and get serious about your studies?*

It didn't matter that Ross got As in English, history and art. According to his father, those subjects had nothing to do with the real world.

You'll never amount to anything if you can't handle finances.

Ross clenched his jaw, wishing he could erase those painful words from his memory, but they seemed etched in place. He focused on the calculator and punched in the numbers once more. When the same answer popped up on the screen, he groaned. Chipping in forty bucks would be easier than telling Adrie he couldn't figure this out.

He reached for his wallet and looked inside. Payday was still a week away. How would he buy gas and groceries if he gave up this money? But what else could he do? With a resigned sigh, he pulled two twenties from his wallet.

The office door creaked and Adrie walked in.

Ross froze, his hand halfway from his wallet to the desk.

Adrie stared at his open wallet. "What are you doing?"

His mouth gaped as his brain scrambled for an answer. "I was…uh…just finishing up the deposit."

She crossed the office toward him. "Why do you have your wallet out?"

Ross tossed the bills on the desk and stuffed his wallet back in his pocket. "I'm just fixing a little shortfall."

She narrowed her eyes. "You were putting money *in?*"

The doubt in her voice hit him like a punch in the gut. "Yes, that's exactly what I'm doing."

"Why? That doesn't make sense."

He huffed and rolled away from the desk. "Because we're forty dollars short."

Her eyes widened. "So you decided to fix the problem by putting in your own money?"

"That's right." He clamped his jaw to keep his irritation under control. He was trying to be sure the store didn't take a loss, and she was upset with him for doing it.

She studied him, conflicting emotions flashing across her face.

He couldn't take her scrutiny any longer. "Okay, the truth is, I didn't want to admit I couldn't figure it out."

"So you were trying to pretend there wasn't a problem?" She turned away and paced to the window.

He circled the desk and followed her. "Come on, Adrie. I probably gave someone the wrong change. I'm just paying the store back for my mistake. Why are you making such a big deal out of this?"

She spun around. "I'm making a big deal because what you did was dishonest. You should've come to me and told me you had a problem, not go sneaking around behind my back and try to fix things...if that's what really happened."

A surge of heat flashed through Ross. She didn't believe him. After all he'd done to step in and take over the store so she could go off and chase her crazy dream.

The door opened wider, and Marian walked in. Her gaze darted back and forth between them. "What's the matter?"

Adrie pressed her lips together and looked away. Ross crossed his arms and did the same.

"What's going on?"

Ross shot Adrie a heated glance. "I came up forty dollars short on the deposit, and Adrie thinks I stole the money."

Adrie gasped. "I did not say that!"

"No? Well that's what you're thinking."

"Since when did you become a mind reader?"

"The minute you started accusing me of stealing money from—"

"Hold on. Both of you settle down." Marian pointed to Adrie. "Now start from the beginning and tell me what happened."

"When I walked in the office, he was sitting at the desk with his wallet open and forty dollars in his hand." She pointed to the two twenties on the desk.

"I told you, I was putting them in the deposit."

Marian picked up the twenties. "Does this money belong to you or the store?"

He shot a glance at Adrie and then looked back at Marian. "It's mine. But that shortfall is probably my fault. I must've given someone too much change."

Marian frowned. "We all work the register, Ross. Why would you assume it's your mistake?"

His face flushed. "I gave out the wrong bills once before, and I didn't realize it until the customer came back. But you and Adrie have been doing this for years. You wouldn't make a mistake like that."

"So you didn't take this money from the deposit?"

Ross straightened and looked her in the eyes. "No. I promise you, I wouldn't do that."

The lines on Marian's forehead eased. "All right. That's good enough for me." She handed him the money. "Put this back in your wallet."

Adrie's eyes bulged. "But, Nana—"

"Honey, he said he didn't take it, and I believe him." She laid her hand on her granddaughter's arm. "We have to trust each other. That's the basic building block of relationships. If we don't have trust, we can't work together."

Adrie crossed her arms. "Trust is earned by being open and honest, not by hiding problems and pretending they don't exist. I won't... I can't deal with that."

Her words hit home, and insight flashed through Ross. To Adrie this wasn't just a foolish mistake or a small lapse in judgment. It was a hurtful offense that brought back painful memories of others who had betrayed her trust, like the previous guy they'd hired to fill this position, and even worse, like her former fiancé.

Regret hit him like a load of bricks tumbling off a truck. Why hadn't he seen this from her perspective sooner?

Closing his eyes, he rubbed his forehead. "I'm sorry. I should've talked to you about the shortfall, rather than trying to cover it up." He lifted his gaze to meet Adrie's. "I let my pride get in the way and make that decision. I won't let it happen again."

Adrie's expression softened.

"Thank you, Ross." Marian smiled, looking relieved. "It takes a lot of courage to admit your mistakes and apologize." She turned to Adrie and nodded, encouraging her to reply.

"Apology accepted," Adrie said, but a wary look still shadowed her eyes.

Adrie leaned on the café counter and watched Ross tuck the deposit in his jacket pocket. Her stomach tensed. There was a lot of money in that envelope—all the cash and checks from the last two days. And after the incident with the forty dollars, she wasn't sure sending him to the bank was the best idea.

A wave of guilt rose and squelched that thought. He had apologized, and she had forgiven him. Still, rebuilding her shaken trust would take time.

"Is there anything else we need while I'm out?" Ross asked.

She continued wiping the café counter. "Not for me."

Her grandma set a stack of books on the table. "Could

you stop by the hardware store and pick up that new handle for the basement door?"

"Sure. I'll swing by B&B's after I pick up my car at the repair shop."

Adrie looked up. "What about Cam's car?"

"I'm picking up Chandra. She's driving me to the repair shop, and then we're trading cars."

Adrie gripped the cloth. Why had he asked Chandra to help him?

"She needs the SUV to pick up Cam and Rachel from the airport tonight. Her Miata is too small."

Adrie's face warmed, embarrassed that he'd read her thoughts. She'd forgotten Rachel and Cam were returning from their honeymoon this evening. Trading cars with Chandra made sense.

"I'm sure you'll be glad to finally get your car back," her grandmother said.

Ross nodded. "I can't believe it took so long to finish the job. I hate to think how much it's going to cost, but I have to have a car."

"Don't worry. It'll work out." Her grandma sent him a reassuring smile. "Now, you better get moving if you are going to take care of all those things and get to the bank before they close."

Ross gave them a playful salute, and headed out the back door. He certainly didn't seem to carry any burden from their confrontation about the deposit shortfall.

Adrie turned on the faucet and rinsed her hands in warm water. *Lord, what if Nana is wrong about Ross? What if he really was trying to steal that money, and he lied to us? He seemed sincere. Should I believe him?*

But how many times had Adam apologized and begged her forgiveness?

She hung the cloth over the side of the sink, and her mind jumped back to those final weeks with her fiancé. His growing hesitation about their wedding plans and his cooling affection should've been clues something was wrong. But she pushed away those warnings and told herself she was overreacting. They were both in their final semester and focused on graduation.

Then one day, she discovered a suggestive text from Marie on Adam's phone. She confronted him, but he said there was nothing going on between him and Marie. He even had the nerve to say she was being paranoid and possessive. She backed down and apologized, sealing it with a kiss and trusting him with her heart.

Two days later, she'd discovered the truth: Marie and Adam had been secretly seeing each other for weeks, and Adam was planning to break off their engagement.

Had he ever really loved her? Had she loved him? She wasn't sure now, and the thought that she might have married someone so untrustworthy shook her to the core. It was a blessing she'd found out the truth about his character before it was too late.

She pulled in a sharp breath, stunned by that thought.

"Adrie? Are you all right?"

She blinked and looked up. "What?"

Nana walked toward her. "I hope you're not still upset about the forty dollars."

She shook her head. "No, not really." In light of those memories, Ross's choice to hide his mistake was a small matter. He'd taken responsibility for it. Her grandmother was right. She needed to give him the benefit of the doubt. He was not like Adam. And she was a fool if she let herself get them mixed up in her mind.

Her cell phone buzzed in her pocket. She pulled it out and checked the screen. The number began with a 612 area code. Minneapolis! She pressed the screen and lifted the phone to her ear with a trembling hand.

* * *

Ross dashed in the rear door and strode quickly through the store.

Marian looked up as he passed. "Back so soon?"

"I got halfway to the Arts Center and realized I grabbed Cam's car key, but I forgot his house key. I need to take in Cam's mail and check his house before he gets back tonight. Got to have those keys."

Marian nodded, but a slight frown creased her forehead as she glanced toward the front of the store.

Were there other customers who needed help? He looked around, but he didn't see anyone except Adrie behind the sales counter. Her back was toward him as she held her cell phone to her ear.

The last time he'd seen that key was this morning when he'd opened the store. Maybe he'd put them by the cash register. He cut through the café and headed for the sales counter.

Adrie closed her cell phone and dropped it in her skirt pocket. She turned and looked at him, her face pale, and her expression somber.

Ross's steps stalled, his keys forgotten. "Are you okay?"

"That was the Minnesota Philharmonic."

His stomach dropped. "What did they say?"

She shook her head. "They don't want me to come out for an audition."

A crazy mixture of elation and frustrations flooded him. "Did they say why?"

"They liked my CD. She said I have a lot of promise, but they have three other applicants with more experience. One who lives right there in Minneapolis, so..." She heaved a sigh. "I guess that's that."

He stepped behind the counter and slipped his arm around her shoulder. The top of her head barely reached his chin, making her seem more vulnerable. He didn't want her to go to Minneapolis, but everything in him wanted to protect her from this kind of hurt. "I'm sorry, Adrie. I know you were hoping this was your ticket out of here."

"Thanks." She leaned against him. "She encouraged me to keep playing and get some more experience." She shook her head. "How am I supposed to do that if no one will hire me?"

"Hey, this is just the first place you applied. It's not the end of the road." He reached down and lifted her chin. "Don't give up yet. You're a gifted musician. You just have to keep playing and working toward your goal."

"I don't know, Ross. What if this isn't the right path for me?"

He studied her face. Was she having doubts because of this setback or because her feelings for him were changing? Hope kindled in his heart. "I'm sure if you keep on praying, the Lord will show you the way."

Chapter Fifteen

Adrie checked her cell phone and reread Ross's latest text message as she walked across the street toward Clarkson's Photography studio.

Help! Kids are out of control. Can you come over and bring your flute?

Adrie chuckled and shook her head. She had no idea why he thought the flute would help, but he sounded desperate, so she'd grabbed her flute case and headed out.

Good thing Irene, Barb and Hannah had been at the bookstore, finishing an impromptu game of Scrabble with her grandmother when Adrie received Ross's text. Irene had offered to stay and help Nana so Adrie could head over to Clarkson's and meet Ross.

Adrie pushed open the studio door, and children's voices greeted her. Her steps stalled. She blinked and took in the chaotic scene.

A harried young woman with short dark hair looked her way. She wore charcoal pants and a black sweater over a bright red turtleneck. A small foam football sailed across the room over her head. She spun around. "Hey, guys, this is not a playground. Put the ball down."

The boy who had caught the ball looked about twelve and

had red curly hair and large hazel eyes. He held on to the ball, but used it to bop a younger boy on the head, while a dozen or so other children moved around the room.

The woman smiled and looked her way. "I hope you're Adrie."

She nodded. "I am."

"Good. Ross said you were on your way." She smiled and offered her hand. "I'm Regina Silverton with the Division of Children and Family Services."

"Adrie Chandler." She shook Regina's hand.

"Another case worker was supposed to come along today, but…as you can see, I'm on my own. It's a challenge to keep kids occupied anytime, but put a dozen of them together in a small room with nothing to do but wait their turn, and you've got a real situation." She chuckled. "But I don't blame them. They're excited about having their pictures taken."

Ross walked into the room bringing back one of the boys from a photo session. His gaze connected with Adrie's. Relief flashed across his face. "Hey. Thanks for coming."

"Sure." She stepped closer and lowered her voice. "I can see why you called in the reserves. How can I help?"

"I was hoping you might give a demonstration or a mini concert—something to keep the kids occupied."

She nodded. "My teacher from Morrowstone is part of a program that brings musicians into schools. I went along and watched them a few times. Maybe I could use some of those ideas."

"Great."

"How many kids have you photographed so far?"

"Four down, nine to go." He grinned. "They're really great kids. Each one has a story. I don't want to rush them through."

Adrie's gaze traveled around the room. The group included eight boys and five girls, who all looked around eight to twelve, although one little girl with long dark curls looked younger. The thought that each one waited for a family made her heart ache. Her parents might be far away, but she knew they loved her and there was a possibility of connection. These kids didn't have that anchor.

She lifted a silent prayer. *Father, please help Ross capture what's special about each child. Let these photos stir the hearts of everyone who sees them. And help these kids find families who will treasure them.*

"Okay, everyone, look up here." Regina clapped her hands to get the children's attention. The children quieted and turned toward her. "I have a surprise for you. Please sit down."

The children exchanged glances and took seats, except for the two oldest boys who leaned against the back wall.

"Michael, Noah, I'd like you to have a seat please." Regina's firm voice and steady gaze won the challenge, and the boys slid down the wall and sat on the floor.

"This is Ms. Chandler. I'd like you to give her your attention."

Adrie's stomach quivered. Watching experienced musicians present a program to children was different than doing it herself. But she sent off another prayer, straightened her shoulders and smiled at the kids. "How many of you have heard an orchestra play? Before you raise your hand, I'm not talking about seeing it on TV, I mean live and in person."

Two girls raised their hands.

"Great. We don't have a whole orchestra here today, but we do have one of the instruments." She took out the three pieces of her flute. "Raise your hand if you know the name of this instrument."

A little African-American girl, who looked about nine years old, lifted her hand. Her hair was styled in neat rows of braids with lavender beads dangling at the ends. She wore a cute purple jumper over a lavender turtleneck.

Adrie nodded to her.

"It's a flute." Confidence filled her voice, and her dark eyes sparkled.

"That's right. Now here's an even tougher question. An orchestra sometimes has up to one hundred musicians. But it's divided into four sections. Can anyone tell me the name of one of those sections?"

The little girl with the braids raised her hand while the other children looked at each other with blank faces.

Adrie nodded to her again.

"The strings, woodwinds, brass, percussion, piano and the conductor. There's six sections, not four."

Adrie grinned. "You're right. Sometimes the piano is considered part of the percussion section, but not always. And if you count the conductor there are six sections. And the flute is part of the—"

"Woodwinds," the little girl said, then giggled and lifted her hand to cover her mouth. "Sorry, I forgot to raise my hand."

Adrie cocked her head. "That's right." How did she know so much about music? Maybe Adrie could ask later. But right now she needed to keep moving or she was going to lose the attention of the boys who were already wiggling near the back wall.

Ross tapped one of those older boys on the shoulder and took him back for his photo session.

Adrie held up her flute. "As you can see, the flute has three main parts. We call them the foot joint, the middle or body joint, and the crown or head joint. This is the lip plate, and this is the tone hole." She put it together, then demonstrated how she held the flute and matched her fingers to the keys. "This is a C scale."

As the notes floated out into the room, the children exchanged smiles.

"Okay, now you know a little about the flute. I'm going to play a few songs for you, and I want you to listen and see how many you recognize." Adrie launched into a series of familiar children's folk songs.

The children leaned forward, watching her, some with mild interest and others with rapt attention. When she finished and lowered her flute, Regina applauded and the kids joined in. The little girl with the braids rose up to her knees and clapped, a smile wreathing her face.

For the next half hour, she kept the kids involved by asking questions and encouraging them to identify the songs. Ross came in and quietly tapped a child on the shoulder every few minutes.

Just as she was about to run out of ideas, Ross returned with the last little girl. "Hey, everybody, we're done taking photos. You all did a great job. How about we give Ms. Chandler a hand for playing her flute for us?" He winked at Adrie, and the kids joined him with enthusiastic applause and a few whistles from the boys in the back.

Adrie took a bow. "Thanks very much. You've been a wonderful audience."

The children stood and began gathering up their coats. Ross walked around the room, talking to each child once more.

Adrie motioned Regina over. "The little girl with the braids, what's her name?"

"Amber." Regina smiled. "Isn't she a sweetheart?"

Adrie nodded. "Has she been in foster care long? What's her story?"

"I'm sorry. I'm not allowed to share much information, but I can tell you this—she's bright and gifted. But I'm afraid most of those gifts won't be developed unless she finds a permanent family."

Someone tapped Adrie on the back, and she turned around.

Amber smiled up at her. "I liked hearing you play the flute."

"Thank you, Amber." Adrie sat down so she could be on eye level with her young friend. "You seem to know a lot about music."

She nodded, making the beads in her hair dance. "My daddy played the clarinet, and my mommy played the piano."

Adrie's throat tightened. What happened to her mother and father? She pushed that thought away. "A love for music runs in your family."

"I took flute lessons at my last school." Her smile dimmed. "But I had to move to a different family. They don't have lessons at my new school." She bit her lip and gazed at Adrie's flute with longing in her eyes.

Adrie's heart clenched. She'd started playing the flute when she was about the same age as Amber. What a shame that this little girl's dream had already been dashed.

"Okay, everyone, time to go." Regina pushed open the studio's front door, then turned to Ross and Adrie. "Thanks again." She lifted her hand and waved.

"Any time," Ross called as the kids filed out. "Wow, if we could harness all their energy, we'd be able to power all the lights in Fairhaven."

Regina smiled. "You're right about that."

"I got some really great photos. Wait until you see them."

Adrie slipped the last piece of her flute in the case and looked up at him. "I knew you would."

He tipped his head and studied her, a question in his eyes.

Her face flushed. She snapped the case closed and turned to grab her coat. "I better go."

"Adrie, wait."

She slowed and turned.

"I didn't have time for lunch. Do you want to grab something to eat before we head back to the store?"

Bayside Books was open until nine. If she didn't eat now, she might not have a chance. But she didn't want to say yes and give him the wrong impression. But he wasn't asking her out on a date. They were just two friends stopping for a bite to eat on their way back to work.

He grinned and lifted his eyebrows. "Mexican. My treat—as a thank-you for rescuing me."

She smiled and nodded. "Sure. That sounds great."

A knock sounded at Ross's apartment door. He broke his gaze away from the photo program on his computer. It was almost seven, and he wasn't expecting anyone this evening. He set his computer on the coffee table and answered the door.

Adrie stood in the hallway wearing a tentative smile and holding a large pizza pan.

The mouthwatering scent of melting cheese and spicy sauce drifted upward. "Wow, that looks delicious."

She held the pan a little higher. "It just came out of the oven, and I don't want to eat the whole thing myself. I thought you might help me."

His eyes widened. "You made it yourself?"

She nodded, and her cheeks took on a soft pink tinge. "It's an old family recipe. We had to make everything from scratch in Kenya, so that's the way I like it."

"Sounds great. Come on in." He couldn't hold back his grin as he led her over to the coffee table and pushed aside his computer. "You can put it right here. I'll go get some plates. Be right back." He headed for the kitchen, his steps light. He grabbed the plates, napkins and two cans of soda. With his hopes rising, he returned to the living room.

Adrie sat on the couch, her gaze focused on his computer screen. "Are those the Heart Gallery photos?"

"Yeah, I was just doing a little editing. You want to take a look?"

"Sure."

He sat next to her and placed the computer on her lap.

"Here you go." He slipped his arm behind her on the couch and settled in next to her.

She slowly scrolled through the photos, commenting about the different children. When she opened the first shot of the little African-American girl with the beaded braids, she stopped and studied it more closely. "Look at her eyes. They're so full of life."

"Yes, she's got something special." He glanced at the pizza. "The smell is killing me. Mind if I go ahead?"

"Help yourself."

He loaded a piece on his plate and took the first bite.

"Regina couldn't tell me much about her, except her name is Amber, and she's very gifted. I talked to her just before the kids left, and she said her parents were musicians."

Ross nodded to let her know he was listening.

"She used to take flute lessons. But she had to move to a new foster home, and they don't have lessons at her new school."

"Too bad. It looks like she was really interested."

Adrie opened the next photo. It showed her kneeling down to say goodbye to Amber. "I didn't know you took this picture."

"Yeah, you were pretty wrapped up in what you were doing."

She grinned. "True." Adrie set the computer aside and reached for a piece of pizza.

"You were great with the kids," he said. "Maybe you could do something like that again."

"You mean play for foster kids?"

He nodded. "Or visit schools, or give kids lessons."

She glanced toward the window, a slight smile at the corners of her mouth. "Maybe I will—someday."

After finishing off three large slices, Ross wiped his hands on a napkin. "That's the best pizza I've ever had. You're an amazing cook."

Adrie laughed. "I bet you say that to all the girls."

His smile faded. "There aren't any other girls making pizza for me—or anything else."

She shifted her gaze away. "Oh…thanks. I'm glad you enjoyed it."

He was pushing it, but she seemed receptive. "Hey, what are you doing Tuesday night?"

She sent him a quizzical look. "You mean tomorrow?"

"Yes." He watched her carefully.

"Well, it's my birthday."

"I know." He couldn't hide his grin.

"Who told you?"

"A little bird named Marian."

She laughed. "I'm having dinner with that little bird."

"I know about dinner. She invited me. I mean after that."

Her eyes widened. "She invited you?"

"Yeah. Hope that's okay."

"Of course. She just didn't say anything to me."

"Oops. Maybe that was supposed to be part of the surprise."

Adrie tipped her head. "Is there another part?"

"Well…since it's your birthday, and you love classical music, I got tickets to hear the Whatcom Symphony at the Mount Baker Theater."

She smiled. "I didn't know you liked classical music."

"I like all kinds of music."

"But will that work with dinner?"

"The concert doesn't start until eight. Marian said we could eat early." He reached over and stacked her plate on top of his. "So, what do you say?"

Her smile was full and warm. "I'd love to go."

"You would? Wow, that's great." He'd been planning this for over a week, ever since he'd heard her birthday was coming up. But he'd prayed and waited, asking the Lord to show him when it was the right time to ask. He lifted a silent prayer of thanks. Finally, it looked like the door to Adrie's heart was swinging open, and he was ready to walk through.

Chapter Sixteen

Adrie added a copy of one of her favorite Christmas books to the window display, then stood back. "Do you think that's too many books?" she asked Ross. "I don't want it to be too cluttered."

He leaned over her shoulder. "Can't tell. Let's go out front and take a look."

She nodded and headed for the door.

"Hey, it's cold out there. Let me get your coat."

"We're just going out for a couple minutes."

"It's okay. I'll be right back." He sent her a quick smile and headed for the office.

"Thanks," she called. He had been so sweet lately. Maybe it wasn't just lately. He'd always been thoughtful and caring. The difference seemed to be, she was finally more receptive to it.

She bit her lip. Was she making a mistake by opening her heart to Ross? He'd never mentioned their kiss on the beach or said any more about giving their relationship a chance to grow. Instead, he'd continued to be a kind and caring friend.

What would she do when it was finally time to leave Fairhaven and say goodbye to Ross?

Her heart clenched, but she pushed those thoughts aside. There was no sense worrying about it now.

Ross returned wearing his jacket and carrying her coat. He held it out so she could slip it on.

"Thanks." She sent him a warm smile.

"You're welcome." He winked and held the door open for her.

He certainly knew how to brighten her day and make her feel special. She might as well enjoy their friendship. For all she knew, it could be years before she found her dream job. Maybe she never would. Perhaps all these closed doors were God's way of keeping her in Fairhaven so she and Ross could be together. Was that God's plan for her?

But what about her music? How could she just toss aside fourteen years of study and preparation?

Autumn leaves swirled down the street on a brisk breeze, pulling her attention back to the task at hand. "I suppose we ought to take down the scarecrows this week." They had won an honorable mention with their harvest display, and it had drawn a few people into the store, but the mums had faded and the gourds and pumpkins looked ready to be tossed.

"I'll take it down Thanksgiving morning, then we'll be ready for Black Friday."

"I could help. I don't have to be over at Nana's to start cooking until about ten-thirty."

"Great. How about nine?"

"That works for me."

"Do you have some Christmas decorations you wanted to put up?"

"We usually buy a fresh wreath from Rebecca's Flower Shoppe and string little white lights around the windows."

"Sounds nice." He glanced up at the cloudy sky. "Maybe we'll even get some snow to put people in the Christmas spirit."

"Oh, please, no snow yet." She rubbed her arms and shivered.

"Ross?" a strong male voice called from across the street.

Adrie and Ross turned as a middle-aged couple stepped off the curb and headed their way. Ross sent her a quick glance she couldn't quite interpret.

The man strode toward them dressed in an expensive-looking black wool coat and burgundy scarf. His thick silver hair was neatly trimmed and combed back in a precise style. The woman scurried along behind him wearing a navy raincoat and a gray knit hat with a floppy brim. Under her arm she carried a black umbrella and small purse.

"Dad. Mom." Ross hustled to meet them at the curb and gave his mother a hug, but he hesitated as he faced his father.

Mr. Peterson stuck out his hand, a slight scowl on his face. "Ross." He shook his son's hand and squinted at the bookstore sign. "This is your store?"

"Yes, sir. Bayside Books." He motioned toward Adrie. "This is Adrienne Chandler. Her grandmother owns the store. She's been training me as the manager." He turned to Adrie. "This is my mom and dad, Sandy and Randal Peterson." He sent her a look that seemed to be a plea for patience or understanding.

Adrie gave them her warmest smile and extended her hand, first to his mom and then his dad. "It's great to meet you. Why don't you come inside and warm up? I'm sure Ross would like to show you around."

"Thank you," his mother murmured.

His father silently examined the storefront, his scowl unchanged.

There was obviously some kind of issue between Ross and his parents. She lifted a silent prayer for Ross and followed him up the steps.

He held the door open for Adrie and his parents, and they all walked inside.

"Why, this is a lovely little store," his mother said with a timid smile. "You have gifts and books, and look, Randal, they even have music."

Ross extended his hand toward the back of the store. "Let's go to the café, and I'll get you some coffee."

As soon as Ross settled his parents at a table, he silently motioned Adrie to join him behind the café counter. "I'm sorry. I had no idea they were coming," he whispered.

"Why are you apologizing? It's nice of them to stop by and see where you work."

"They didn't just stop by. They live two hours away in Tacoma."

"Then they made a special trip. That's even more impressive."

"Right." He lifted his eyes to the ceiling. "It would've been nice if they'd let me know they were coming."

"True, but they're your parents. I suppose they thought it would be okay."

"I'm sure this was my dad's idea." He pulled two coffee cups off the shelf. "He's not happy about me working here, and I'm sure he'll make that clear."

She laid her hand on his arm. "Don't worry. I can handle it." She slid open the glass door on the bakery case. "Do you think they'd like the blueberry cinnamon scones or the lemon raspberry squares?"

"Bring a couple of each. My treat." Ross reached for his wallet.

"Don't worry about it, Ross."

"No, I'll gladly pay for anything to keep my father happy." He put the bills in the cash box and poured two cups of coffee.

Adrie carried the bakery treats to the table. "Here you go." She passed out the plates, forks and napkins.

"Thank you." His mother looked up and smiled at Adrie,

her eyes a tired watery brown. His father's frown faded
slightly as he eyed the desserts.

Ross placed the coffee, cream and sugar on a tray. He had
been praying about his relationship with his parents, but he
hadn't expected them to come to the store unannounced. As
he headed to the table he debated asking Adrie to join them,
because his father's comments were often abrupt and critical. He wanted to protect her from that if he could. He set
the tray on the table and forced a small smile.

"Sit down, Ross. Your mother and I want to talk to you."

He sent Adrie an apologetic glance.

She nodded slightly and slipped away to the other side of
the store.

Ross took a seat. "I didn't know you were coming to
Fairhaven today." He tried to keep his tone even, but it carried a hint of frustration.

"We're on our way to Shawn and Andrea's. They invited
the whole family up for Thanksgiving." His father narrowed
his gaze.

Ross's stomach burned. "Mom mentioned that when she
called last week, but I didn't know you were going up three
days early." His father usually resisted taking extra time off
work, even for holidays.

"Your mother wants to help Andrea get the nursery
ready." Ross's sister was due to give birth in early December. The baby would be his parent's first grandchild, and
even his father seemed to be interested in the preparations,
which was totally out of character.

His mother leaned forward. "Won't you please come with
us?"

He held back a groan. So this was why they'd stopped in.
He pulled in a deep breath. "I'm sorry, Mom. I only have
Thursday off, and I don't want to spend most of the day driv-
ing back and forth to Andrea's."

"But Julie and Peter are coming. And it's so rare we can all get together." She glanced around the store. "It doesn't look like you're very busy. Couldn't someone else handle things for a few days?"

He shook his head. "We're expanding our hours for holiday shopping, and we're pulling in extra help. I can't take time off right now. I thought I explained that last week."

His father huffed and crossed his arms. "I told you that we'd be wasting our time coming up here."

"Randal, it's not a waste of time to come and see where our son works."

His father scanned the bookshelves, and his scowl deepened. "Are those Bibles?"

His mother's eyes widened.

Ross's stomach knotted, but he straightened his shoulders. "Yes, this is a Christian bookstore."

"You mentioned going to church, but I had no idea you'd taken a job at a…a religious store." His father's face flushed. "What were you thinking, Ross?"

Marian approached their table. "Hello. You must be Mr. and Mrs. Peterson." Her gracious smile gave no hint if she'd heard his father's comments. "I'm Marian Chandler, the owner of Bayside Books."

His father rose and shook her hand. "Mrs. Chandler."

"Oh, please, call me Marian." She turned to his mother. "I can't tell you how pleased we are to have Ross working with us. He's wonderful with our customers, and his technical skills are finally bringing our store into the twenty-first century." She chuckled. "He's got us all set up with a new inventory system, email promotions and now we're even using social networking. We feel very blessed that he's managing things for us."

Both his parents' expressions eased as they listened to Marian's praise. He would definitely have to thank her later.

Adrie looked around the end of the bookshelf. "Ross,

sorry to interrupt, but could you give me a hand for a minute?"

"Sure." He turned to his father. "Excuse me. I'll be right back." He got up and followed Adrie across the store. "Thank you," he whispered.

She looked over her shoulder. "I really do need your help. The register is frozen, and all my usual tricks aren't working."

"Okay. I'll take care of it."

"How's it going with your parents?"

Ross shook his head. "Not too well. They just realized this is a Christian bookstore, and my father's about to pop a blood vessel."

"They didn't know?"

"No, I didn't tell them." He stepped behind the sales counter and pressed a few keys on the register. "My parents won't discuss faith or religion. They never have. I've been praying for them, but there hasn't been any great breakthroughs yet."

"I'm sorry, Ross. That must be hard." Her tone was soft and filled with understanding.

He clenched his jaw. "They're good people. Maybe that's the problem. They don't see their need for God."

"It might help if you spent more time with them."

"They wanted me to go with them to visit my sister and her husband. That's why they're here."

"You mean for Thanksgiving?"

He nodded. "Andrea lives almost three hours north of Vancouver—definitely too far for a day trip. But I guess they thought if they came up here and asked me in person, I might change my mind."

Adrie laid her hand on his arm. "I'm sorry, Ross. I didn't know you wanted time off."

"No, it's okay. I told them I couldn't go last week. They just don't like to take no as an answer."

"Well, most families get together for Thanksgiving."

"True, but I'd rather spend the day with you." Marian had invited him over, and he'd been looking forward to celebrating with Adrie, her grandmother and friends. He'd even promised to bring a pumpkin pie. His plans were set. He didn't want to change them.

But what about his family? How would they hear about God's love if he didn't spend time with them and live it out in front of them?

"Maybe you could smooth things over by offering to come down for Christmas." Warmth and compassion shone in Adrie's eyes. "I'm sure if we planned ahead, you could take time off that week."

A slow smile returned to his face. "That's a good idea." It might satisfy his parents. And maybe, just maybe, if things continued to move ahead as he hoped, Adrie would come along with him.

His spirit lifted as he imagined her there with him, enjoying time with his sisters and their husbands. Andrea's baby would've arrived, and that would brighten everyone's holiday.

Yes, Christmas in Tacoma was sounding better all the time.

Chapter Seventeen

Adrie held her breath as the strains of Vivaldi's Second Symphony rose to the final crescendo. The music was so beautiful she felt like her heart would burst. The last note sounded and held for several seconds, then the conductor turned and bowed. Applause broke out across the Mount Baker Theater auditorium. Adrie and Ross quickly joined in.

She leaned closer to Ross, hoping he could hear her words above the crowd's response. "That was fantastic."

His grin spread wider and his dark eyes glowed. "So you liked it?"

"Are you kidding? I loved it." She often listened to classical CDs and practiced her flute most days, but it had been at least seven months since she'd attended a live performance.

He slipped his arm around her shoulder. "I am glad we could come tonight."

"Me, too." She smiled up at him, enjoying the possessive drape of his arm around her. Sharing the evening with Ross had been the perfect way to end her birthday celebration.

He glanced at the program. "Looks like there's a ten-minute intermission. Would you like to walk out to the lobby?"

"Sure. I'd love to take a look around." She had only been

in the theater twice since it had been remodeled. She lifted her gaze to the elaborate Moorish dome and ornate chandelier in the center of the ceiling. How many hours had it taken the workmen to refurbish it to its original 1927 elegance? They walked out to the mezzanine, passed the beautifully carved columns and descended the stairs to the main floor lobby.

"I'll be back in a couple minutes." Ross wove his way through the crowd toward the water fountain and men's restroom. She stepped up next to the unusually tall mirror-backed chairs against the lobby wall. The theater was considered an architectural treasure with its lovely dark wood ceiling and unique furniture and fixtures. Even the EXIT signs looked like they were specially designed with unique Moorish style lettering.

"Adrie?" a feminine voice called.

She turned and searched the crowd. Charity Holmes, a friend from the Western Washington University orchestra, waved and crossed the lobby toward her.

Adrie greeted her with a hug. "It's good to see you. When did you get back?

"Just last night."

"I'm sure your family is happy to have you home for Thanksgiving."

Charity nodded. "I'm glad I live close enough to drive up for the weekend."

"How are things going with the Oregon Symphony?"

Charity lifted her eyes to the ceiling. "Amazing. I love Portland. It's such a great city. I've made some good friends. I'm sharing an apartment with one of the other violinists." She took a step closer to Adrie, and her expression sobered. "I heard what happened between you and Adam."

Adrie's heart lurched. She knew word of her broken engagement had spread among her friends, but most of them were kind enough not to mention it. But Adam also played in the Oregon Symphony. Had he told Charity the same stilted version he had shared with several other friends?

"I'm so sorry," Charity continued. "You must've been devastated."

Adrie squared her shoulders and met Charity's sympathetic gaze. "It was hard at first, but as my grandmother says, it's better to find out a person's true character before you say, 'I do,' rather than after."

"That's for sure." Charity lowered her voice. "Did you hear he and Marie broke up?"

Adrie's throat tightened, and she had to force out her words. "I'm not really in contact with either of them."

Charity leaned closer. "Well, Marie found out he was flirting with the orchestra's associate librarian, and she confronted him. He denied it, but she didn't believe him. And after everything that happened with them and you, it's no wonder she didn't trust him."

A spurt of elation flashed through Adrie, but it quickly faded. "I'm sorry. It sounds like they're both suffering for their poor choices."

"That's very generous considering how they treated you." She patted Adrie's arm. "So, what's new with you? Are you still helping your grandmother at the bookstore?"

"Yes, but we hired a new manager to take my place, so I've been looking for auditions."

Charity's expression brightened. "Hey, one of our flutists has to go back to Idaho to take care of her mother."

Adrie's pulse quickened. "Are they looking for subs to fill in for her?"

"No, she's giving up her position."

Adrie blinked, her mind spinning.

"The auditions are in a couple weeks. But I'm sure there's still time to apply. Oh, wouldn't it be great if we could play together again? And Candice and I are looking for another roommate to share the apartment. You could stay with us."

The Oregon Symphony had a wonderful reputation. But how would she feel playing in the same orchestra with her ex-fiancé? She bit her lip and then slowly shook her head. "I don't know, Charity. I'm not sure auditioning there would be a good idea."

Her friend sent her a knowing look. "Hey, this is a great opportunity. Don't let the fact Adam is there hold you back. It might be awkward at first, but you'd get over that in a little while." Charity squeezed her hand. "Oh, please say you'll at least apply."

Before she could answer, Ross returned.

Adrie's stomach tightened. She hoped Charity wouldn't say any more about the opening in Portland. She wasn't even sure she wanted to apply, and if she did, being hired was a long shot. Why upset Ross with that possibility?

Adrie introduced Ross to Charity, who batted her eyelashes and extended her hand. "Hello, Ross."

He smiled and shook her hand. "Nice to meet you, Charity." They talked for a few more minutes about the concert and their Thanksgiving plans.

"I better get back to my seat." Charity gave Adrie a quick hug. "I'll talk to a few people and email you if I hear anything else."

Adrie forced a smile. "Okay. Thanks. Enjoy the time with your family. Say hello to everyone for me."

"I will." Charity flashed a final smile at Ross, then turned and walked back into the auditorium.

"Ready to go back to our seats?" Ross asked.

She nodded. He placed his hand on her lower back and guided her through the thinning crowd. The warmth of his hand sent a pleasant sensation through her, reminding her how much she enjoyed being with Ross.

What would he say if he knew about the opening in Portland? If she did apply and received an invitation to audition, would he encourage her to go, or would he ask her to stay?

* * *

Ross lifted the fragrant evergreen wreath and placed it on the nail next to the bookstore's front door. The florist had added a bright red bow, holly sprigs and pinecones. He cocked his head, checking the position. "It looks a little too close to the door. Maybe I should move it. What do you think?" When Adrie didn't answer, he glanced over his shoulder.

She stood on the sidewalk, nibbling on her thumbnail and staring off down the street.

"Adrie?" He reached for her and lightly touched her arm.

"What?" She blinked and looked up at him.

"You seem like you're a million miles away." He couldn't keep a hint of frustration out of his voice.

"Sorry." She shifted her gaze back to the storefront.

"Do you like the wreath there?"

"It looks okay. What do you think?"

He sighed. "I just said I thought it was too close to the door."

"Oh, go ahead and move it. Whatever you think is fine with me."

He mustered a half smile, then took her hand and gently pulled her down on the front step next to him. "What's going on, Adrie?"

She frowned slightly. "What do you mean?"

"I've been trying to carry on a conversation for the last twenty minutes, but you haven't heard half of what I've said."

"I'm sorry. I've just got a lot on my mind right now."

"Such as?"

She looked away for a few seconds, and then turned back. "Remember my friend Charity, the one we talked to last night at the concert?"

"Sure. She was the friendly blonde with the eye problem."

"Eye problem?"

"Yeah, she was always looking up at me and fluttering her eyelashes."

Adrie's lips tilted up, and she bumped his shoulder with hers. "Come on. Be serious."

He stifled his chuckle, glad to see her smile, even if just for a moment. "Go on."

"Charity plays violin in the Oregon Symphony." She lifted her gaze to meet his. "One of their flutists is leaving. They're looking for someone to replace her."

He clenched his jaw, determined not to let his conflicting emotions show on his face. She had been waiting and praying for this opportunity for a long time. It was important to her, just as important as opening his photo studio again was to him.

Steeling himself, he forced out his next words, "Are you going to audition?"

"They're only scheduling auditions for the top three candidates."

"But you're going to apply?" He held his breath. Maybe she'd say no. Maybe she didn't really want to leave him and move so far away.

She nodded. "But I've learned my lesson. I'm not going to let myself get so emotionally invested like I did with Minneapolis. There's lots of competition. I've got to be prepared for this to be a long process with some rejections before something finally opens up."

He pressed his lips together and watched the tattered leaves tumble down the street.

"At least Portland is closer than Minneapolis." She fiddled with the hem of her jacket. "If it works out, I could drive home to Fairhaven sometimes."

He doubted that. Portland was at least a four-hour drive without any traffic, and the area between Seattle and Tacoma was notorious for delays. Once she got settled and made new friends, trips to Fairhaven would probably be few and far between.

Why was he getting so worked up? Even if she auditioned, what were the chances she'd get the position?

His spirit sank a few more feet. Who was he kidding? Adrie was beautiful, talented and eager to move ahead with her career. Once they met her and heard her play, the decision would not be difficult.

Like a knife in his chest, the truth sank in—as much as he wanted to ask her to stay, he couldn't do it. He would not be the destroyer of her dreams.

It was time to prepare himself to say goodbye.

Chapter Eighteen

Adrie carried a plate of pumpkin cheesecake squares into Nana's dining room and placed it on the buffet. She smiled as she looked at the beautiful flower arrangement her grandmother had made using colorful mums and peach-colored roses. Hand-painted Pilgrim figures stood on one side of the arrangement and a set of turkey salt and pepper shakers stood on the other.

Adrie loved the way her grandmother decorated for every holiday. It was a fun tradition, and it had inspired her to start her own collection.

Nana stepped into the room with a large apple pie. She placed it next to Irene's colorful fruit tart. "Look at these lovely desserts. I can't wait to try one of your pumpkin squares."

"I used your recipe," Adrie said.

"I'm sure they'll be delicious." She leaned over and kissed Adrie's cheek. "I'm so proud of you, honey, for so many reasons." Her grandmother's eyes shone with approval and tenderness.

"Thanks, Nana," Adrie said, hoping she could always live up to her grandmother's hopes for her.

Preparing Thanksgiving dinner with Nana had been a

treat. But she wasn't the only one on hand to help. George arrived before noon, bringing extra folding chairs. Nana put him to work scrubbing and peeling potatoes, while Adrie snipped green beans and finished decorating the top of the seven-layer salad. Ross arrived around one, eager to lend a hand. Her grandmother passed him the potato masher, and he whipped the big pot of spuds into shape in no time. When the turkey was roasted to a golden brown, Nana removed it from the oven and handed George the carving knife and fork.

Adrie's eyes misted. Grandpa Bill had always carved the turkey. Nana and George exchanged a tender glance, then he set to work slicing the bird.

After dinner, Adrie's gaze traveled around the table, her heart and her stomach both full. The laughter and lively conversation of these dear friends had brightened the holiday and raised her sagging spirits. And having Ross seated next to her made the holiday complete.

George sat beside Marian, along with his brother-in-law, Ray, and Ray's wife, Claudia. Ross sat next to Ray, and the two had spent a good part of the meal talking about photography and all the best scenic spots in Whatcom County.

Irene sat on the other side of the table with her adult grandson, Alex. Nana's friends Hannah and Barb sat next to Irene, along with Les Hawkins, their mailman.

It was a tight squeeze to fit everyone in, but Adrie had never been happier. These dear friends seemed as close as family, and since her parents and brother were so far away, it was wonderful to have them join their celebration.

Her grandmother beamed a bright smile. "All right, who's ready for dessert?"

Adrie helped pass out plates, then returned to her place next to Ross.

He glanced at her overflowing dessert plate. "Looks like you had a little trouble making up your mind."

She sent him a playful smile. "I thought I should try a little of each dessert. I don't want to hurt anyone's feelings."

"Good idea." Ross lifted his fork and took another bite of his pumpkin cheesecake square. "These sure are delicious."

"Thanks."

"Oh, you made them?" He sent her a teasing grin.

She laughed and gave his shoulder a playful bump. "You know I did."

"In that case I better have another one." He got up to refill his plate.

Nana's phone rang. "Oh, I hope that's the kids." She rose from her chair and strode into the kitchen. A few seconds later she leaned her head out the kitchen doorway. "Adrie, it's your parents."

Adrie's heart leaped, and she hurried to join Nana. With the time difference and challenge of making an international call, she didn't get to talk to her parents on holidays very often.

Nana handed her the phone. "Here you go, sweetie."

"Thanks, Nana." For the next few minutes Adrie shared the latest news, first with her mom and then her dad. She'd emailed them about not making the cut for the Minneapolis audition, but she gave them the rest of the story. Then she told them about meeting Charity at the concert and the opening in Portland.

"That's great you have a friend there," her father said.

She bit her lip, debating if she should tell him Adam also played with the Oregon Symphony, but she decided against it.

"So did you apply for this new position?"

"Not yet, but I plan to work on my letter tonight. I have a CD and résumé ready, so I should be able to mail it tomorrow."

"Good. Your mom and I will be praying about it. Might be just the right spot for you. Portland isn't too far from

Fairhaven. I'd much rather have you there than all the way across the country. At least you'd be a bit closer to your grandmother."

"I'm trying not to get my hopes up. I'm sure a lot of people will apply."

"True. But you've got talent, honey. And you've worked hard for a long time. I think that will pay off soon. Just keep praying and trusting and let's see what God will do."

Adrie smiled. "Thanks, Dad." It had been a while since she'd received such encouraging words from her father.

"You're welcome, honey. And remember, Mom and I love you. We'll be proud of you no matter what job you decide to take. The most important thing is that you're following the Lord and serving Him with your whole heart. That's what really matters."

Tears misted her eyes, and she had to swallow before she could answer. "That's what I want, too."

"Then you'll be fine. Just fine. Keep praying and trusting, honey."

"Okay, Dad, I will."

"That's my girl."

She blinked a few times. "I love you, Dad."

"I love you, too. Now go enjoy your holiday." Her father chuckled. "Sounds like you have a houseful today."

"We do. It's been fun, but I wish you were here."

"Me, too, but at least we got to talk on the phone this time."

"I'm glad you finally got through." She talked to him for a few more minutes, then finished her call and hung up the phone. She pulled a tissue from the box on the counter and walked back into the dining room.

Ross looked up as she returned to the table. "Good call?"

She nodded. "One of the best."

He tipped his head, questioning her with his eyes.

"I haven't talked to my dad for a few months, so that was special."

He slipped his arm around her shoulder. "I'm glad."

"What about your parents?" she asked. "Are you going to give them a call?"

He frowned slightly. "I guess I should."

"It would probably mean a lot to them."

With a thoughtful nod, he got up from the table and pulled his phone from his pants pocket. "You're right. Might as well take care of it now."

"Wait." Adrie got up. "Maybe we should pray first."

He hesitated a second. "Okay. Thanks."

She led him into her grandmother's sunroom, then clasped his hand and bowed her head. She slowed her breathing and focused her thoughts. "Father, please give Ross an extra measure of love and patience as he talks to his family today. Soften their hearts and help them see who You really are. Please draw them closer to each other and to You."

After a few seconds, he tightened his grip on Adric's hand. "Lord, I want to build a stronger relationship with my family, and I want to help them get to know You. Please help me forgive them for past mistakes. I know You can change their hearts, because You changed mine. I trust You to do that for my family, too. Thank You." He released a deep breath. "Amen."

"Amen," Adrie added, then smiled up at him, her heart warmed by his honesty and trust.

How could she have doubted his faith? His commitment ran deep, and it drew her to him in a stronger way.

Adrie bit her thumbnail and carefully read through her résumé one last time. Her life and training were summed up on those two pages, and there was a lot more white space than type. Was it enough to impress the decision makers at the Oregon Symphony? A nervous quiver passed through her stomach.

"Let it be enough, Lord," she whispered, then hit Print and leaned back on the couch. She lifted her hand and rubbed her tight neck and shoulders as her printer hummed and churned out her letter and résumé.

Maybe a cup of chai would soothe her jangled nerves. She walked into the kitchen and spotted the large plate of leftover desserts on the counter. One more pumpkin cheesecake square tempted her.

A knock sounded at her apartment door, and her heart leaped. It was a little late for Ross to drop by, but she couldn't think of a better way to end the day. Spending time with him would be much more comforting than a cup of chai or a rich dessert. She hurried to the door and pulled it open.

Adam Sheffield stood in the hallway.

She gasped, then blinked to make sure her eyes weren't playing tricks on her.

"Hi, Adrie." He tipped his head and sent her a charming smile, looking pleased that he'd surprised her.

"Adam, what are you doing here?"

"I'm in town for a few days, and thought I'd drop by and say hello." His gaze traveled over her with a slight lift of his eyebrows. "You look great."

Her stomach clenched, and a warning flashed through her. She needed to keep her guard up against his flattery. "How did you get in downstairs?"

"It was unlocked. I didn't think you'd mind if I came up."

She did mind, but it seemed rude to put it that bluntly. "I'm sorry, Adam. It's late. This isn't a good time for a visit." She stepped back and reached for the door handle.

"Hey, it's not even ten o'clock, and it's a holiday weekend."

"Shh!" She glanced toward Ross's door, hoping he hadn't heard Adam.

"What are you worried about?"

"I don't want to...bother my neighbors." She lowered her voice. "We're opening early tomorrow. I need to call it a night."

"Ah, come on, Adrie. Can't you spare a few minutes for an old friend?"

Was he being loud on purpose? She glared at him. "Keep it down."

He leaned toward her and lowered his voice. "No one would hear us if you'd let me in."

All kinds of reasons why that was a bad idea raced through her mind, but inviting him in would be better than Ross discovering her talking to her former fiancé in the hall-way. "Okay, but just for a minute."

He stepped past her into the apartment and glanced around, a slight smile on his lips. "Looks like things haven't changed much around here."

Adrie closed the door and crossed her arms. "You're wrong, Adam. A lot of things have changed, including me."

He chuckled as he walked toward the couch. "Oh, Adrie, you're always so serious."

Irritation flashed through her.

"You should lighten up and enjoy life a little."

"I enjoy life just fine, in spite of the fact that my former fiancé betrayed my trust and broke our engagement."

His expression faltered. "How many times do I have to apologize before you forgive me?"

She closed her eyes. "I can't believe we're having this conversation again. What do you want, Adam? Why are you here?"

He studied her for a moment and released a resigned sigh. "There's an opening for a flutist with the Oregon Symphony. I wanted you to know."

She shot a quick glance at her open computer on the coffee table.

A slow smile spread across his face. "You already heard?"

She hated that she couldn't keep a secret from him, while he had always been adept at hiding the truth from her.

"Are you going to apply?" A hopeful light sparked his dark brown eyes.

"I'm considering it."

"I've got some influence. I'll put a good word in for you."

"Please don't. If I get an audition, I want it based on my abilities, not anyone's influence."

He clicked his tongue. "You're still mad at me, aren't you? That's why you won't let me help."

She released an exasperated huff. "Adam, do you have any idea how much you hurt me, let alone how much money I had to pay to cancel our wedding? We're talking about thousands of dollars."

His shoulders drooped. "I knew you were upset, but I didn't think about the money."

"Well, you should have. I'm still paying off those bills."

He met her gaze. "I thought helping you get the position in Portland might make up for…everything that happened."

"Don't bother."

He tipped his head, looking slightly hurt. "What can I say? What do you want me to do?"

A genuine apology would've been nice. But he didn't have a clue.

He walked toward her holding out both hands. "Come on, Adrie, can't you give a guy a break? I didn't mean to hurt you. I just got carried away. It was only that one time."

Those excuses were not enough to change her mind about Adam Sheffield. She turned, walked toward the door and pulled it open. "Goodbye, Adam."

He stared at her for a moment, confusion and a hint of hurt in his eyes. "Bye, Adrie," he said as he walked out.

She closed the door, leaned back against it and shut her eyes. "Thank You for protecting me from making the worst mistake of my life."

Ross set aside his guitar and walked toward the kitchen. As he passed the front door, voices in the hallway caught his attention. It was awfully late for someone to be visiting Adrie. He cocked his head to listen. One of the voices was distinctly male.

He ought to check on her and make sure she was okay. But what if it was Eric, the chef, or some other guy she had invited over? All the more reason to step out the door and make sure he knew Adrie had someone watching out for her.

Would she appreciate it or think he was sticking his nose in where it didn't belong? He turned and stalked into the kitchen. It was none of his business who Adrie invited over. She hadn't made any promises to him. But he hated knowing some guy was over there with her.

He spun around, marched to the front door and jerked it open—just as her apartment door closed. He strode down the hall, past her apartment and descended the stairs.

Glancing through the window, he scanned the rainy parking lot. His car sat next to Adrie's white Echo under the lone light. Two spaces down, raindrops bounced off the hood of an unfamiliar silver BMW. He stepped outside and looked around to be sure her late-night caller hadn't made a quick exit down the street, but he didn't see anyone.

The chilled air stung his nose. Raindrops spattered his shoulders. He shoved his hands in his pants pockets and huffed. What was he doing standing out in the rain? This was crazy. He looked up at Adrie's apartment. Shadows flickered across the glowing curtain drawn over her window.

Who was up there with her?

He clenched his jaw and trudged back inside. As he closed the door, a chill traveled up his back. He lowered his head and closed his eyes, trying to summon up a prayer, but no words came.

He was losing Adrie—either to another man or another job. It was time he faced that reality and got on with his life.

Chapter Nineteen

"Do you have any Christmas cards in yet?" A harried young mother balanced a fussy infant on one hip while she tried to hold the hand of her wiggly preschooler.

Adrie smiled and nodded. "Sure. Let me show you what we have."

Though it was just past ten o'clock, more than a dozen customers browsed the bookstore aisles, taking advantage of the Thanksgiving weekend sales. The scent of fresh brewed coffee and apple cinnamon muffins floated toward Adrie as she led the young mother through the store. "Here are the boxed cards, and we have individual cards in the display rack." She pointed them out and patted the preschooler on the head. "Let me know if there's anything else you need."

As Adrie walked back to the sales counter, her thoughts shifted to Ross and she frowned slightly. He'd been unusually quiet this morning. At first she thought it was the early hour, but now she wasn't so sure. Even when several customers lined up to pay for their purchases, carrying coupons from his email promotion, his somber mood didn't lift.

She couldn't think of anything she'd said or done on Thanksgiving to upset him. In fact, it had been a wonderful day. She'd never felt closer to him. It didn't make sense.

Glancing around the store, she spotted him in the Bible section patiently listening to an older man talk about a trip to Israel he'd taken twenty years ago.

She slipped behind the sales counter and straightened a stack of calendars.

Ross joined her and rang up the older gentleman's sale. "Have a nice weekend," he said as he sent him off, but his words didn't carry their usual enthusiasm.

Maybe he just needed some friendly encouragement. She turned to him. "It looks like your email with the twenty-percent-off coupon was a big hit."

"Yep." He fiddled with the stack of ten-dollar bills in the register drawer.

"We've already done more business today than we did all last week." Surely that would make him look her way and smile.

But he stepped over to the computer and clicked through to the distributor's website, then made a note on a yellow legal pad.

She drummed her fingers on the counter, trying to come up with something else to help him out of this funk.

His cell phone rang. He pulled it from his pants pocket and answered.

She should step away and give him some privacy, but she stayed put instead, hoping his conversation might help her figure out what was bothering him.

"Hey, Regina." A slight smile pulled at one side of his mouth as he listened. "Thanks. I'm glad you like them." He paced to the other end of the sales counter. "Well, I hope it helps the kids. That's what's important."

An image of the foster children bouncing around in the photo studio flashed through Adrie's mind, making her smile. It sounded like Regina was happy with the photos.

Ross looked up and met her gaze. "Yes, she's right here. Would you like to speak to her?" He hesitated, listening to

Regina again. "Yes, I will. Thanks." He held out the phone to Adric. "She wants to talk to you."

"Thanks." She took the phone and greeted Regina.

"I wanted to thank you again for coming over on picture day." Regina laughed softly. "I'm not sure how I would've kept the kids busy and held on to my sanity without your help."

"I enjoyed meeting the kids and sharing my music."

"They certainly loved your presentation...and that's why I'm calling. Do you remember Amber, the little girl who answered so many of your questions?" Her tone hinted at some problem.

Adrie's stomach tensed. Had something happened to Amber? "Of course. Is everything all right?"

"She had to move to a new foster family, and it's been a rough transition for her."

Adrie's heart sank. "I'm so sorry."

"We hated to move her again, but we really had no choice." Regina was quiet for a moment. "I had an idea I wanted to run by you, something to help Amber."

Adrie's heart stirred. "What did you have in mind?"

"Amber used to take flute lessons, but with these last two moves she had to stop."

"Yes. She mentioned that when we met."

"I wondered if you could spend a little time with her and perhaps give her a flute lesson."

Adrie leaned against the counter and smiled. "I'd love to." She talked to Regina for a few more minutes, and they set a time for Adrie to meet with Amber.

"Thanks, Adrie. I really appreciate it. I'm sure this will put the sparkle back in Amber's eyes."

"I hope so. Please tell her I'm looking forward to seeing her." Adrie ended the conversation and handed the phone back to Ross. "Remember Amber?"

Ross nodded, his expression wary.

"Regina wants me to give her flute lessons."

"Did you say yes?"

She nodded. "We start next Wednesday."

He frowned slightly. "You should be careful."

"What do you mean?"

"You don't want to make a promise you can't keep."

She straightened. "I'm not."

"Didn't you just apply for the position in Portland?"

"Yes, but that's a long shot. I don't even know if I'll get to audition."

"But you might. And if you promise Amber lessons, and then can't give them, that's going to hurt her more than if you'd never started."

Heat flooded her face, and she lifted her chin. "I wouldn't hurt Amber, and I don't intend to break my promise."

He sent her a doubtful, pained look. "I hope not."

She grabbed a stack of postcards and tapped them on the counter to straighten the pile. "I don't see why I should have to put my life on hold just because I have my résumé out there."

"This is not just about you, Adrie. It's about a little girl who's been through a lot of pain and disappointment, and I'm just saying you should be careful about the promises you make."

His words sliced through her heart, and she turned and strode out of the sales area.

Amber sat on the edge of the kitchen chair, swinging her legs back and forth in time to the music as Adrie played her flute.

Adrie lowered her instrument. "Now you try it."

Amber raised the borrowed flute to her lips, pulled in a deep breath and launched into the A scale.

Adrie nodded and sent Amber an encouraging smile. For a first lesson, it was going extremely well. Amber was an eager student who listened carefully and easily remembered how to finger the notes.

Amber lowered her flute and looked up expectantly.

Adrie clapped. "Bravo! Good job."

She smiled and ducked her head, soaking up the praise like a little sponge.

A knock sounded at Adrie's apartment door. She glanced at the clock. How could an hour have gone by so quickly? "I think that's Ms. Silverton."

Amber groaned. "Oh, it can't be time to go yet."

Adrie answered the door and greeted Amber's caseworker.

"How did it go?" Regina asked in a hushed tone.

"Great." Adrie turned to her young student. "We had a good visit and a very productive lesson."

Regina smiled and nodded. "I'm so glad." She crossed the living room and stood beside Amber's chair. "Okay, it's time to go. Please get on your coat and hat."

The little girl looked up with pleading eyes. "Do we have to go now? We were just getting to the good part of the music."

Regina placed her hand on Amber's shoulder. "I'm glad you enjoyed your time with Ms. Chandler, but I promised I'd get you home in time for dinner."

"Do we have enough time for me to put the flute away?"

"Sure, that would be fine."

Amber opened the case, then slowly took the flute apart and carefully wiped each piece before she placed it in the red velvet padding. Finally, she closed the case and secured the two latches. Her lip quivered as she held the case out toward Adrie. "I liked playing your flute. Thank you for the lesson."

Adrie knelt in front of her. "You know, I don't use this flute very often. It usually just sits on the shelf in my closet. Would you like to take it with you?"

Her eyes widened. "Really? I can take it home?"

"Sure, if you promise to take good care of it and practice every day."

"Oh, I will. I promise." She lunged forward and wrapped her arms around Adrie's neck. "Thank you."

Adrie's throat tightened and she had to force out her words. "You're welcome, sweetie."

Amber stepped back, her eyes glistening as she hugged the flute case to her chest.

"Why don't I hold on to the flute while you get your coat?"

"Okay." Amber passed Regina the case and dashed off toward the hall.

Regina's gaze followed her. "You've just made her a very happy little girl."

"I hope it's okay to give her the flute."

"It's very generous. Thank you."

"Could she come next week for another lesson?" Adrie asked.

Regina beamed. "I was hoping you'd offer. I'll speak to her foster mom and get back to you."

"This is a good time for me, but if there's a conflict, let me know and maybe we can change it."

"All right." Regina hesitated. "What you're doing…it's very special. I know it means the world to Amber."

"I love teaching someone who's so eager to learn."

Amber hurried back into the room wearing her puffy red jacket and red-and-white-striped knit hat pulled down at an odd angle. She grinned up at Regina and held her hands out for the flute case. "I can carry it now."

Regina returned her smile. "Okay, here you go." She turned back to Adrie and held out her hand. "Thank you. I'll be in touch."

"It was a pleasure." Adrie shook Regina's hand then

leaned down and gave Amber a hug. "Take care, sweetie. Have fun with the flute, and I'll see you next week."

Amber gave her another tight hug.

Adrie showed them to the door and waved to Amber once more as she took Regina's hand and walked down the stairs. As she stepped back into her apartment a warm sense of satisfaction settled over her heart.

Amber might have enjoyed the lesson, but Adrie was the one who felt blessed by the time she'd spent with the little girl. She closed her eyes and whispered a quiet prayer, "Thank You, Father. Thank You so much."

The cold December wind swirled around Ross as he hustled down the street, headed for Tony's Coffee House. He sank deeper in his coat, wishing he'd remembered to grab his scarf before he'd left the bookstore. As he rounded the corner at Twelfth and Harris Streets he bumped into George coming the other way.

Ross grinned and grabbed his arm. "Hey there, buddy, better watch where you're going."

George laughed and slapped Ross on the back. "Good morning to you, too. Where are you headed?"

"Over to Tony's for some java. Want to join me?"

"Tempting. Very tempting." He glanced down the street. "I need to be over at the studio by ten, but I have a few minutes."

"Great." He and George set off at a brisk pace. "Marian mentioned you're going back to Seattle soon to spend Christmas with your family."

"That's right. I'll be leaving on Friday."

Marian and George usually saw each other several times each week. Ross glanced over at George. "Will you be coming back in January?"

George nodded. "I've got to square away a few things and look into putting my house up for sale in the spring."

He winked at Ross. "But of course that all depends on how things continue to develop with Marian."

"I see." Ross grinned, happy to hear George had serious intentions toward his employer. Ross had grown very fond of Marian, and he felt a sense of responsibility for her.

"We've talked about where our relationship is headed and possibilities for the future, but I haven't proposed yet, so keep this under your hat."

"I won't say anything." It would be hard to keep it from Adrie, but he understood why George wanted to surprise Marian.

"I know most women consider the proposal very important," George continued. "And I want to do it right, for Marian's sake. I'm thinking Valentine's Day would be a nice time to pop the question. What do you think?"

Ross fingered his cell phone in his pocket. What did he know about proposing? He couldn't even convince Adrie to take their friendship to the next level. "Sounds good to me."

"I can stay with Ray and Claudia again when I come back after Christmas. But I hope our wedding won't be too far off in the future." George released a contented sigh. "Maybe in the late spring or early summer."

Ross shoved his hands deeper into his pockets. It must be nice to know where your relationship was going and feel confident the woman you loved, loved you back. Ross exhaled and pushed those thoughts aside. "I'm happy for you, George. I hope it works out just the way you planned."

"Thanks, Ross." They arrived at Tony's Coffee House. George pulled open the door and motioned Ross to go ahead.

Ross stepped inside, and warm, coffee-scented air greeted him. Bayside Books Café coffee was good, but some mornings he took the short walk to Tony's for something special. He ordered a large caramel macchiato, then took his steaming cup and sat at one of the tables by the window.

George joined him. "I'm glad we ran into each other. Ray

and I were talking last night, and I wanted to let you know what he said."

"Okay."

"Ray was a judge for the *Washington Trails* magazine photo contest." George looked at Ross over the top of his glasses. "He was quite impressed with your entries."

Ross sat up straighter. "Thanks. I didn't know Ray was a judge." He hadn't heard anything since he'd sent the prints off two months ago.

"This is his sixth year." George glanced around and back at Ross. "I'm not supposed to tell you, but he gave you a very high score. Of course it has to be averaged in with the other judges' numbers, but I wouldn't be surprised if you were a finalist, maybe even the winner."

Ross's chest expanded. "Wow, that would be nice."

George cradled his coffee cup in his hands. "He was pleased with the Heart Gallery Project photos, too. You really captured something special with each of those kids." He leaned forward and lowered his voice. "Ray thinks you've got what it takes to run the studio."

Ross's pulse jumped, and he set down his coffee cup. "What do you mean?"

"He's talked about retiring for years, but last night was the first time he sounded serious about selling the business. I'm not sure how much he's asking, but I thought you should know he's open to you buying him out."

Ross's hopes sank like a rock dropped in a pond. "It sounds like a great opportunity. But I can't afford to buy his business."

George held up his hand. "Don't dismiss the idea outright. Ray's pretty well set. He wouldn't need all the money up front. Maybe you could work out some kind of deal."

Ross sat back and rubbed his chin. If he owned his own studio again, he could do what he loved every day. He'd also be able to show his father he could be a successful businessman.

But what about his promises to Adrie? If he took over Ray's studio, she would be back at square one—stuck in Fairhaven, searching for a manager to replace her and locked out of her dreams. Ross clenched his jaw. He couldn't do that to her. It wouldn't be right. Not after all the time she'd invested in training him.

He slowly shook his head. "I appreciate the fact he's flexible, but even if I had the money, I couldn't pull the rug out from under Adrie like that. She's got her name out there, and she's hoping to hear from the Oregon Symphony any day."

"But what if that doesn't work out? What if she stays in Fairhaven?"

Ross's chest tightened. "I wish she would, more than anything. But she's got her heart set on playing her flute, and she can't do that here, at least not full-time in an orchestra the way she wants."

George steepled his fingers. "What about you, Ross? What about your future? A chance to buy an established business like this doesn't come along every day. Ray's built a good reputation. He'd let you keep the Clarkson name if you want."

Ross stifled a groan. How could he turn this down? It would take years for him to rebuild his business without the help of someone like Ray. But hurting Adrie would be a high price to pay.

"Why don't you at least talk to Ray? See what he says. Then you could make your decision based on facts."

Ross tightened his grip on his coffee cup. He wanted to do what was best for Adrie. But wasn't there some way they could both have what they wanted? Did he really have to sacrifice his dream for hers? And if he did, where did that leave him—tied to a job he'd hoped was temporary and without the woman he loved?

Chapter Twenty

Adrie carefully placed her flute back in the padded case and glanced across the platform at Ross. He slipped his guitar strap over his head and held his guitar with one hand as he talked to one of the other guitarists on the worship team.

The spotlight shone down on him, highlighting his dark hair and strong facial features. The moss-green sweater he wore accentuated his broad shoulders and athletic build. He was a handsome man. She'd always known that, but she couldn't seem to take her eyes off him tonight.

She'd waited all day for him to suggest they ride to worship practice together, but the invitation never came. She'd driven to church alone, and spent the whole time trying to figure out why he was pulling away. During practice he'd only acknowledged her once with a brief half smile.

Was he still bothered because she'd promised Amber flute lessons when there was the remote possibility she'd be invited to audition in Portland?

"Adrie?" Geoff Swenson stepped into her line of vision.

She blinked and looked up. "What? Sorry, I didn't hear what you said."

Geoff grinned and glanced at Ross. "I noticed."

Adrie's face flamed.

"Here's a copy of the new song we'll be introducing in two weeks."

"Thanks." She stashed the papers in her folder. "I'll take a look at it this week."

"Thanks. See you Sunday." Geoff moved on to distribute music to the others.

Ross placed his guitar in the case and latched it closed. Without looking Adrie's way, he walked off the platform and picked up his coat from the front pew.

Adrie grabbed her flute case and followed him. "That was a good practice. I liked your intro on that last song."

He glanced at her, then looked down and frowned slightly as he zipped his coat. "Thanks."

"Did you get your copy of the new song Geoff wants us to learn?"

"Yeah, I got it."

She bit her lip, her heart aching at the distance she felt between them.

He looked up and met her gaze with a mixture of tenderness and regret in his eyes.

Her heart sank. "What is it, Ross? What's wrong?"

He quickly shuttered his expression. "Nothing." But rather than walking away, he stood waiting for her.

She quickly pulled on her coat. "Do you want to stop for coffee on the way home?"

A look of relief flashed in his eyes, and his expression eased. "Okay."

They walked out of the sanctuary together, and he held the front door open for her.

The cold wind whistled around her and blew down her neck. "Brr, it's freezing out here." She tucked her hand in the crook of his arm.

He leaned toward her. "I'll keep you warm."

She snuggled in closer, wanting to restore that sense of

connection between them. She needed Ross. She counted on his lighthearted comments and constant encouragement to lift her spirit and help her focus on what was good and right in the world. These last few days, he'd kept her at arm's length, and it had been a painful wakeup call.

As they crossed the parking lot, her steps slowed and she glanced up at the sky. "Look how bright the stars are tonight."

He lifted his eyes. "You can even see the Milky Way."

His warm breath fanned across her cheek. She shifted her gaze from the stars to his familiar profile, and she held on to his arm a little more tightly.

"Why don't we take my car?" he said.

She nodded, pleased that he suggested riding together. "Okay."

"Would you like to go to Skylark's?" He opened the door for her.

"That sounds good." She slid into the seat and smiled her thanks as he shut the door. Ross's friendship was a special gift, and she never wanted to take it for granted.

He climbed in and started the car. As they pulled out of the parking lot, Adrie's cell phone rang. She retrieved her phone from her purse. An unfamiliar number with a Bellingham area code flashed on the screen. She lifted the phone to her ear and answered.

"This is Evelyn Johnson, from St. Joseph's Hospital. Is this Adrienne Chandler?"

She frowned. "Yes, this is she."

Ross shot her a questioning glance, then returned his focus to the road.

"Marian Chandler arrived by ambulance a few minutes ago. She asked us to call you."

Adrie's stomach dropped, and she clutched the phone. "What happened?"

"She fell at home. The doctor examined her, and she's on

her way to X-ray now. She may have some broken bones. She wanted us to let you know."

"All right. Thank you. Please tell her that we're on our way." Adrie's mind spun as she tapped the screen to end the call.

"What's going on?"

"That was St. Joseph's Hospital. Nana fell. She's in the E.R."

Ross pulled in a sharp breath.

"Can you take me there?"

"Sure." Ross set his jaw, turned right at the next street and took the entrance to the 5 Freeway north. He accelerated and moved to the left lane.

Adrie gripped the door handle and lifted a silent prayer. *Please let her be okay, please.*

Ross made the trip to St. Joseph's in less than seven minutes. He pulled into the E.R. parking lot and took the first open spot. They jumped out of the car and dashed into the hospital.

After a brief wait, they were ushered into the curtained exam room where Adrie's grandmother lay on a bed with a white sheet pulled up to her chest. She looked pale and fragile, and a pillow and folded towels rested around her right arm.

"Oh, Nana." Adrie rushed to her grandmother's side and clasped her uninjured hand. "Are you in pain? What does the doctor say?"

Nana gripped her hand, and a look of relief washed over her face. "I'm so glad you're here." Tears glistened in her eyes.

"Of course we're here. Everything's going to be all right." Adrie sent Ross a worried glance. Her grandmother seemed so vulnerable and shaken.

Ross stepped up next to Adrie. "They said you fell. Tell us what happened."

Nana sighed and gave her head a weary shake. "I wanted to put some ornaments near the top of the Christmas tree, so I pulled my kitchen stool into the living room. One minute I was reaching up there, then the next I lost my balance and fell off the stool."

Adrie cringed. "And you were all by yourself. I'm so sorry."

"It's my own fault. I should've waited until you came over, but I was prideful and sure I could do it myself."

"Don't be so hard on yourself, Nana."

"I know better than to climb up on a stool like that. You know what they say, there's no fool like an old fool." Her grandmother's eyes filled and she looked away.

Adrie bit her lip and glanced at Ross.

"It's all right, Marian," Ross said. "Accidents happen to everyone."

She sighed. "You're right. I'm sorry. This pity party is not doing me any good."

"It's okay, Nana. What does the doctor say?"

"I have a broken wrist and a possible concussion. I want to go home, but they said I need to stay overnight for observation. I'm just waiting for a room."

"Okay, I'll stay with you," Adrie said.

"No, I want you to go home and get your rest. You and Ross have to take care of the store."

Adrie wanted to argue, but she didn't want to upset her grandmother. "All right, but I'm not leaving until you're settled in your room."

Nana gripped her hand again. "As long as it's not too late." She shifted her gaze to Ross. "You'll be sure she gets home safely?"

"You have my word on it." He laid a comforting hand on Adrie's shoulder. "We'll stick around until you're set for the night."

Adrie looked up into his eyes, and thankfulness flowed from her heart. What would she do without Ross?

Adrie held tightly to her grandmother's good arm as she guided her up the steps and into her house late Sunday afternoon. "Take your time, Nana. We're not in a hurry."

"Maybe you're not, but I can't wait to get home again." Nana grimaced and held her injured arm close. "Three days in the hospital is too long for me."

"They would've let you out sooner if you'd been good." Ross grinned and winked at Adrie as he followed them into the house carrying Nana's small overnight bag.

Her grandmother chuckled. "I suppose you're right. I did keep those doctors and nurses hopping."

"Where would you like me to put your bag?"

She nodded toward the hall. "My bedroom is the second door on the left. Put it up on the bed. That'll make it easier for me to put things away."

He nodded and headed down the hall.

"I'll put your things away for you, Nana. Why don't you sit down and rest." Adrie slipped off her coat, then helped her grandmother.

Nana looked pale and tired. She wore a sling to protect her right arm, which was in a cast, and sank down in her favorite spot at the end of the couch. Adrie quickly hung up their coats. She planned to stay with her grandmother as long as she needed her. And her first goal was convincing Nana to take a nap.

Ross returned to the living room. "What else can I do for you, Marian?"

"Would you mind bringing in the mail?"

"No problem. I'll be right back."

Ross had been a wonderful help. He'd worked extra hours so Adrie could spend part of each day with Nana at the hospital. He'd managed the store practically on his own and done a terrific job. Today he'd driven Adrie to church, taken her out to lunch and then gone with her to bring Nana home. She could've managed without him, but it would've been much more difficult.

Now if she could just help her grandmother regain her strength, perhaps the weight she had been carrying would lift off her shoulders.

Adrie headed into the kitchen to make her grandmother a cup of tea, and her cell phone rang. She hurried back to the living room and pulled it from her purse. The unfamiliar number began with a 503 Oregon area code. Her pulse jumped, she tapped the screen and answered.

"This is Martha Warrenton, personnel manager with the Oregon Symphony. Is this Adrienne Chandler?"

She gripped the back of her grandmother's wing chair. "Yes, it is."

"We received your application. Are you still interested in the flutist's position?"

"Yes...I am."

"We're holding the audition here in Portland on December 16."

Adrie swallowed. "December 16?" That was only four days away.

Martha Warrenton hesitated. "I'm sorry this is such short notice. We made our initial selection over a week ago and invited three candidates, but one of them isn't able to come. So we reviewed the applicants, and decided to extend an invitation to you."

A ripple of uneasiness traveled through Adrie. She hadn't been a first-round pick. What did that say about her chances? "I appreciate the invitation. I'll look forward to meeting you." She forced enthusiasm into her voice, but wasn't sure she sounded too convincing.

How could she leave town this Thursday? The timing couldn't be worse.

Ross returned with the mail and handed the stack to Marian.

Adrie walked toward the kitchen as Martha Warrenton gave her a few more details about the audition and promised to follow up with an email. Adrie thanked her, finished the call and slipped the phone into her pocket.

"Everything okay?" Ross asked.

Her stomach tightened into a painful knot as she turned to face him.

He stood in the kitchen doorway, questions reflected in his dark eyes.

The flicker of excitement she'd felt during the call faded. "That was a woman from the Oregon Symphony. They want me to come down for an audition."

He tensed. "When?"

"This Thursday." Her chin quivered and tears gathered in her eyes. "How can I go to Portland and leave Nana here all by herself? And what about the store? This is our busiest time of year. How are you going to manage by yourself?"

He frowned and shifted his weight to the other foot. "Don't worry about the store. I can handle it." He rubbed his jaw. "Maybe we can ask one of Marian's friends to stay with her."

"But it's almost Christmas. I'm sure they're all busy."

"I can hear you in there, making plans without me," Nana called.

Adrie took a deep breath and walked into the living room. "Sorry, Nana. I didn't mean to leave you out of the loop." She sat next to her grandmother.

"I know, dear." Nana patted her knee. "Now, there's no need to worry about me. Barb or Irene will stay with me. They love to hover like mother hens. I'll be just fine." She reached for Adrie's hand. "Go to that audition and give it your best."

"Oh, Nana." Her voice broke as she reached over and gave her grandmother a gentle hug.

Ross cleared his throat. "I'll make some calls. See if I can line up a few more people to help at the store."

Adrie sniffed and sat back. "Thank you, Ross."

"No problem." He quickly turned and strode out the door.

Adrie pressed her lips together as she watched him go. A tear overflowed and spilled down her cheek.

"Oh, honey, why the tears?"

"I'm just not sure this is the right thing."

"We'll be fine. Don't worry. Ross is an excellent manager, and I'm on the mend."

Adrie clasped her hands in her lap. "I know. What I mean is I'm not sure I should go to the audition."

Her grandmother sat back. "But this is your chance to have what you've always wanted. Why this sudden change of heart?" She looked toward the door and back at Adrie. "Is it because of Ross?"

Adrie swallowed. "Partly. The thought of leaving him is just… I don't even want to think about it."

Nana sent her a sympathetic smile. "Do you love him?"

Adrie lifted her gaze to meet her grandmother's. "I could, if I let myself."

"Have you told him how you feel?"

She shook her head. "I said I only want to be friends, and I'm afraid he believes me."

"Why don't you just tell him what's in your heart?"

"And what if I do? Does that mean I give up my chance to play professionally?"

"But to say goodbye to someone you love? Is it worth that much to you?"

She closed her eyes, trying to make sense of her jumbled thoughts and emotions. "I know God's given me a gift. And when I play, I feel a deep sense of connection with Him, like that's what I was born to do. How can I give that up?"

"No one's saying you have to give up your music."

"I know, but that's not the only issue." Adrie's heart clenched. "Ross has never said he loves me, and he's never asked me to stay."

Nana clicked her tongue. "Maybe he's holding back because he knows how much your music means to you."

Adrie groaned and laid her head back on the couch. "What am I supposed to do, Nana? I'm so confused."

"I'm not sure, honey, but God knows. He has a plan just for you." Nana laid her hand on Adrie's arm. "Why don't we pray and see what He says?"

Adrie sighed, rubbing her eyes, feeling tired and discouraged and definitely not in the mood to pray. "You really think that will help?"

"I *know* it will. Then you just need to be watching and listening for His answer."

A tiny spark of hope ignited in her heart. Maybe Nana was right. Maybe God could help her make sense out of all these decisions if she would just take time to stop and ask Him. She bowed her head. "Okay, Nana. Let's pray."

Ross trudged down the steps and out to his car, feeling like fifty-pound weights were chained to his feet.

Adrie was leaving. He knew it was coming. He should've been prepared, but the news hit him hard, like someone had kicked him behind the knees and knocked him down. With a low growl, he climbed in his car and slammed the door.

Closing his eyes, he leaned forward and rested his head on the steering wheel. *Lord, what am I supposed to do? I love Adrie. I don't want her to go. But I can't ask her to stay. She's been working toward this her whole life. But just thinking about sending her off is killing me.*

He pulled in a deep breath and tried to think clearly. *He loved Adrie.* So that meant he should do what was best for her. Holding on to her or begging her to stay would just cause more pain for both of them. He wouldn't hurt her like that.

Another shaft of pain sliced through his chest. He not only had to let Adrie go, he needed to encourage her and send her off with his best wishes for the future.

He sank lower in his seat. *Lord, there's no way I can do that on my own. You're going to have to help me.* He waited there a few more minutes, silently praying and asking God for strength.

Finally, he reached for his phone and tapped in Ray Clarkson's number. As he waited for the call to go through competing thoughts fought in his mind. Ray picked up after the third ring.

"This is Ross Peterson. I wanted to get back to you about the photo studio." He gripped the phone and forced out the next words. "I appreciate your confidence in me, but I'm not going to be able to follow through on that offer."

"I'm sorry to hear that, Ross. I was hoping we could make a deal."

"So was I."

"If the rate of the buyout is too steep, I'm open to changing the terms."

"No, your offer is more than generous."

"Not sure what I'll do now. George doesn't want to keep things running too much longer. If you don't want the business, I suppose I'll have to shut it down and put the building up for sale."

Ross gritted his teeth and held back a groan. All that equipment, all those contacts and years of goodwill down the drain.

"Are you sure about this, Ross? If you need more time, I could give you a few more weeks to think it over."

"No, I need to stay at Bayside Books. With Marian out of commission, they need me more than ever."

"George told me about Marian's fall. How's she doing?"

"We brought her home from the hospital today, but the doctor wants her to stay off her feet for a few weeks."

"Good thing she has you and Adrie to manage the store."

Ross shook his head. "Adrie just got invited down in Portland for an audition. She's leaving on Thursday."

Ray huffed. "That puts you in a real spot. How are you going to run things without her?"

"I don't know. I'll figure something out."

"I admire you, Ross, keeping your word to Marian and holding down the store for her while Adrie's away. George told me that she wants to play in a symphony. Do you think she'll get that position?"

He hesitated, wishing he could give a different answer. "I'm afraid she will, Ray."

Adrie sank down on the stool behind the bookstore sales counter, kicked off one shoe and rubbed her sore toes. She had spent too many hours on her feet the last few days. And her toes weren't the only problem. A slight headache had been inching its way up her neck during the last half hour.

Had she eaten lunch? She glanced at the clock. It was already past two—definitely time for a break and some nourishment. She reached for her cup of chai, took a sip and grimaced. Cold chai was not going to do the trick.

"I'll be right back," she called to Ross.

He stood in the biography section, shelving a box of books. "Take your time," he said without looking her way.

She walked toward the café. Though she prayed about her decision every day, she didn't sense a clear answer or reason to change course. She and Ross had worked side by side all week, but the only comment he had made about her trip to Portland was on Tuesday, when he had asked if she wanted him to bring in her mail. She stared at him for a few seconds, trying to absorb the fact that he didn't seem to care she might be leaving Fairhaven for good. With a stiff nod, she thanked him, then excused herself to cry in the bathroom.

Thinking of it now, her head pounded harder, and her stomach felt like she'd swallowed a rock. Here she was on the eve of the most wonderful opportunity of her life, and she'd never felt more miserable.

But her plans were set. Tomorrow morning at seven, she'd load her car and head to Portland. She'd called Charity and told her that she was coming to audition. Her friend was thrilled and invited her to stay through the weekend. Adrie agreed, hoping she might hear the audition results while she was there.

"Hello, sweetie." Irene smiled at her from behind the café counter. "Can I get you something?"

"Would you stick this in the microwave?" She passed Irene her cold cup of chai.

"Sure thing." Irene placed it in the microwave and glanced over her shoulder at Adrie. "Everything okay?"

"I'm exhausted. I've been running like a crazy woman all week."

"Getting ready for your big audition?"

Adrie nodded, but she couldn't summon up a smile.

"Well, you sure look pretty today. I love that royal-blue sweater. It makes your eyes sparkle like sapphires."

A slight smile lifted the corners of her mouth. "Irene, you are so sweet."

"Well, it's true, and I think a certain someone agrees with me." She wiggled her eyebrows and tilted her head to the left.

Ross walked down the aisle toward the café.

Adrie leaned toward Irene. "Shh, you don't want to embarrass me, do you?"

Irene's eyes grew large, and she quickly covered her mouth to hold back a giggle.

Ross stepped up next to Adrie. "What's going on?"

"Nothing." Irene grabbed a cloth and began vigorously wiping the counter.

Ross sent her a quizzical look. "Could you pour me a cup of coffee?"

"Coming right up." Irene reached for Ross's mug.

He turned to Adrie. "You want to sit down for a minute?"

"Do you think Mandy is okay up front?" They'd just hired the young woman two days ago.

"I told her to holler if she needs help."

"Okay. I could use a break." Adrie took her chai and a banana nut muffin and walked over to the table in the corner.

Ross sat across from her. "So, are you ready for your trip to Portland?"

Her hand stilled, and she looked up at him. "I finished packing last night."

He nodded, his expression revealing nothing. "Good."

Good? He thought it was good she was ready to leave? Her heart chilled a few more degrees.

"Did you hear they canceled the Christmas Boat Parade last weekend because of the storm?"

She bit into her muffin and shook her head. It tasted like sawdust in her mouth.

"They rescheduled it for tonight at six. I was thinking I'd drive down to the bay and watch." He took a sip of his coffee. "Would you like to come?"

She blinked and almost choked on her bite of muffin. "That sounds fun."

"Is that a yes?"

"Can Mandy and Irene stay until seven?"

He nodded. "They're both here until closing."

Maybe this was the answer to her prayer, and Ross would finally share what was in his heart. "Okay. I'd love to see the boat parade."

His expression brightened. "How about we pick up some pizza to take along?"

She smiled and nodded. "I'd like that."

Three hours later darkness cloaked Fairhaven, and stars twinkled overhead. Adrie held the warm box of pizza on her lap as Ross drove toward the bay. She glanced over at him, and bittersweet memories filled her mind. How could she have known him for only four months? It seemed much longer. They'd spent a lot of time together, and that had drawn them closer. But it was more than that. Ross understood her past and how that had shaped her. He'd taken time to discover what she liked and what was important to her. When she needed someone to talk to, he was always there.

How could she drive away tomorrow into a future without him?

But that was exactly what was going to happen, and he didn't seem inclined to stop her. Tears stung her eyes and she quickly looked away.

Ross pulled into a parking spot near the Taylor Avenue Dock. "I think we can see pretty well from here."

She pushed her troubled thoughts away, determined to enjoy this precious time with him. "This is perfect. Ready for some pizza?"

"More than ready." He turned toward her, his eyes glowing with some undefined emotion.

She passed him a couple of napkins, then opened the box and offered him first pick. The scent of sausage and pepperoni drifted up and made her mouth water. "This was a great idea."

He grinned. "You mean the pizza or the boat parade?"

"Both." Her throat clogged, and she had a hard time swallowing her bite.

"Look, here they come." A sailboat drifted by with colorful lights strung from the top of the mast to the bow and stern and all around the riggings.

Adrie leaned forward. "It's so pretty."

The first boat sailed on and another soon followed. This

one had white lights in the shape of a star on top of the mast and strings of lights leading down to a manger scene on the deck.

"Wow, that one's nice," Ross said between bites.

Adrie nodded, savoring her pizza and the twinkling lights, but most of all just being with Ross.

"So what was Christmas like in Kenya when you were growing up?"

Memories came flooding back, and she turned to him with a smile. "We had the whole month of December off from school so we could travel home and spend that time with our family. My mom would decorate the house and bake lots of cookies. Then the week before Christmas, we'd drive up to the mountains and cut a small pine tree."

"You're kidding. They have pine trees in Kenya?"

She chuckled and nodded. "We made paper birds and stars to decorate the tree, and sometimes we cut out pictures from Christmas cards to make ornaments. Then on Christmas Day we exchanged handmade gifts, and we went to church where they had a pageant and acted out the Christmas story. It was a simple celebration compared to what people do here, but I loved it."

"Sounds nice."

"I'm blessed. My parents and brother are far away, but I'll always have those memories. Now Nana and I have our own fun traditions."

"Like what?"

"We're busy at the store right up to Christmas Eve, but we always close early enough so we can go to the candlelight service at church. Then we have a special breakfast together on Christmas morning and exchange gifts. After that we call my family and a few other relatives. Then we just relax and enjoy the day. In the evening we usually watch *It's a Wonderful Life* or *While You Were Sleeping*."

Her smile dimmed. How often would she see her grandmother if she moved to Portland? She might be able to drive home for holidays, but everything about her daily life would change. She'd have to find a new church and get used to a new job with all its pressures and expectations.

Ross reached for her hand. "I'm glad we can share tonight. Sort of a nice way you can add to those Christmas memories."

She wove her fingers through his and tears stung her eyes. This might be her first and last Christmas season with Ross.

The boat parade sailed on for another thirty minutes. They finished the pizza and Adrie set the empty box on the car floor.

When the last boat floated out of sight, she shifted in her seat and turned toward him. Her pulse sped up. Maybe now he'd finally tell her what was in his heart. Surely if he loved her, he'd say he didn't want her to go.

With a sad smile, he reached for his keys. "I better get you home. You have a big day tomorrow. You need to get a good night's sleep so you can do your best at the audition."

Go ahead, tell him that you love him. Say it! But the words stuck in her throat.

They drove home in silence, and when he pulled into the parking lot behind the store, she felt like her heart would break. He was a great friend, probably the best she'd ever had, but he didn't love her. If he did, surely he wouldn't let her go. Not like this. Not without a word.

She pushed open the door and climbed out before he could circle the car and open it for her. She reached back and grabbed the empty pizza box and her purse.

"Here, let me take that." He held out his hand for the pizza box.

She passed it to him, then watched him walk over and toss it in the trash. This was her chance to walk away and not face another painful goodbye, but she couldn't do it. Not yet.

He walked back toward her, and without a word he

slipped his arms around her, pulling her close. "I'll miss you, Adrie."

She held on tight, her heart breaking.

He leaned back and looked into her eyes. "I'll be praying for you and asking God to help you do your best."

She pressed her lips together and nodded. Words were impossible.

Then he leaned down and gave her a featherlight kiss on her forehead, like a dear friend saying goodbye.

Ross paced across the living room, then turned and strode back toward the kitchen. He was going to wear a path through the carpet at this rate. The apartment was dark except for one small lamp that glowed on the end table, and a faint light from a half moon shone through the window.

He'd gone to bed just after ten, but sleep wouldn't come. In just a few hours, the woman he loved was leaving town and most likely changing the course of her life forever.

Was it fair to send her off without telling her the truth? If she knew he loved her, would she change her mind? Why hadn't he told her when he'd held her in his arms? The words had rushed through his mind, begging to be set free, but he'd held back, determined to do what he thought was best for her. Now he wasn't so sure.

But if he spoke up, and she turned down this opportunity, how would she feel later? Would the constant shadow of regret hang over their relationship, making her wish she'd stayed true to her plans? Would she grow to resent him?

If she really cared for him, she wouldn't leave him like this, would she?

Maybe he was a fool to think she could love someone like him—a man with a failed business, an empty bank account and an unknown future.

He sank down on the couch and lowered his head into his hands. *Lord, I thought I heard You speaking to me through*

Cam and George. I've tried to follow that advice and be a good friend to Adrie. I really thought her heart would soften and she'd come around, but she's leaving tomorrow. What am I supposed to do now?

He waited, listening for direction, but the only sound he heard was the steady beat of his heart drumming in his ears. After a couple more minutes of silence, one truth rose and filled his mind. If he loved Adrie, then he had to let her make this decision on her own. His role was to pray and send her off with encouraging words.

He released a deep sigh, letting go of his desire to keep her close and have her for his own. Closing his eyes, he hung on to the truths that anchored his soul—God was still in control. He knew what was best, and Ross was determined to trust Him no matter what happened.

Rising from the couch, he walked to his desk and grabbed a pen. At least he could write her a note and tell her she would always have his friendship and a very special place in his heart.

Chapter Twenty-One

Adrie pulled her keys from her purse and unlocked the trunk of her car. Her hand stilled as she looked up at the pale pink eastern sky. Silver frost dusted the branches of the fir trees at the end of the parking lot. She took a slow deep breath, receiving the beauty of the morning as a comforting gift, but her heart still ached.

Somehow she had to find the strength to get in her car and drive to Portland. With a quiet shake of her head, she lifted her suitcase into the trunk and closed it with a gentle thud. She took the scraper from the glove compartment and started the car. Her hand shook slightly as she grasped the plastic scraper and slid it over her frosty windshield.

If only she could clear away the painful, icy coating covering her heart.

She'd prayed again this morning, but no new revelation came. Her grandmother's words from their last conversation rose in her mind. *If the Lord hasn't given you any new direction, then just follow the last thing He told you. Trust Him, honey.*

A bakery truck rumbled down the street. The wind whistled under the back eaves. She shivered and zipped her jacket higher, then placed her flute case, computer bag and a tissue-stuffed gift bag for Charity in the backseat along with her purse.

Climbing in the car, she closed her eyes. *Lord, You've opened this door for me, and I'm willing to walk through it. But my heart is so heavy. Please give me the strength I need. I'll go and do my best, and leave the decision up to You. But if this is not Your will, and You have another path for me, please show me. I'd turn around in a minute if You make it clear I should be going a different way.*

Lifting her gaze to Ross's dark window, she wished the light would come on and he'd lean out and beg her not to go. But he was probably sound asleep, unaware that she was driving away with a broken heart.

She brushed one last tear from her cheek and drove out of the parking lot. For the next hour she continued to wrestle, pray and beg God to give her peace and clarity for her future.

As she approached Everett, she noticed her fuel gauge was close to E, so she pulled off the interstate. A few blocks from the exit she found a gas station and drove up to the pump. She hopped out and opened the back door. As she lifted her purse, an envelope slid off the backseat and dropped to the floor. Her name was printed on the front in Ross's familiar handwriting.

Her breath caught in her throat, and she reached for the envelope. With trembling fingers, she carefully opened it and pulled out a note card with a photo of a beautiful purple starfish on the front. She bit her lip and read the message.

Dear Adrie,
I wanted you to know I'm praying for you as you go to the audition. I'm sure you'll blow them away when you play. They would be crazy not to hire you on the spot and give you the chance you deserve and have worked toward for so long.

I am proud of you for your determination to see your dream come true. I feel honored that God would call me to fill in for you at the bookstore so you can be free to follow that dream.

But I would not be a true friend if I didn't tell you that saying goodbye and sending you off is the hardest thing I've ever done. I love you, Adrie, with all my heart. And it's because of that love that I can wish you well and pray you will find God's very best for your life.

Until then, know that you have a friend who treasures you.

You'll always have my love,

Ross

Tears flooded her eyes. He wasn't sending her off because he didn't love her. He was releasing her because of his love.

Her heart swelled. She blinked to clear her eyes and read the note once more, letting the tender words soothe and comfort her. Then she noticed an arrow at the bottom, encouraging her to turn the card over and read the back.

I wanted to give you this early Christmas present. Maybe it will remind you of that morning on the beach when we shared our first kiss.

Ross

Pushing aside her computer case, she spotted the small rectangular box wrapped in silver paper and tied with a slim red satin ribbon.

Her heart began to pound as she slipped off the paper and opened the box. She gasped and smiled through her tears. Inside, lying on a bed of soft cotton, was a lovely silver necklace interspersed with aqua sea glass beads and silver charms—starfish, seagulls, fish and clamshells. The design was exquisite and obviously handmade by a jewelry designer. She fingered the beautiful beads, each one tumbled by the sea to a unique shape and size. She lifted it to her lips and closed her eyes.

The words of the card were beautiful, but the necklace declared his love in an even deeper way. *Thank You, Lord.*

Her phone chirped, alerting her to a message. She pulled it from her purse, hoping it might be Ross. But her grandmother's name flashed on the screen. She lifted it to her ear and listened to the voice mail. "Call me, honey. As soon as you can." Adrie tapped the screen and called her grandmother.

"Nana, are you all right?"

"Yes, I'm fine. But I spoke to George this morning, and I think you should know what's going on."

Adrie's stomach clenched. "What do you mean?"

"Ray wants to turn over his studio to Ross, but Ross turned him down."

"Because of the bookstore?"

"Yes, but mostly because he didn't want you to miss out on this opportunity in Portland."

"Oh, that crazy guy, what is he thinking?"

"He's thinking he loves you, and he doesn't want to let you down."

"But he shouldn't give up a chance like this. He's an amazing photographer. Having his own studio again, that's his dream. That's what he's been saving for."

"Exactly, and he's willing to give that all up for you. If that doesn't prove he loves you, then I don't know what would."

"He gave me the sweetest card and a beautiful necklace." Adrie's voice choked off.

"I guess you don't have to wonder about his feelings anymore."

"No, he's made them pretty clear."

Her grandmother waited a few seconds. "I just thought you should know before you get too far down the road."

"Thanks, Nana. It means a lot." She ended the call and slipped the phone back in her purse. Then she picked up the necklace and ran her fingers over the silver clamshell.

Ross glanced at his watch. Had Adrie reached Seattle yet on her way to Portland? Was the weather still clear or had those icy road conditions he'd read about online slowed her down?

This morning just after seven he'd stood at his bedroom window in the dark and watched her pull out of the parking lot. Had she found the card and gift he'd left in the backseat? He checked his phone again, but there were no missed calls, messages or texts.

So much for baring his soul and proclaiming his love.

He lowered himself onto the stool behind the sales counter and stared out the bookstore's front window. It was going to be a long four days. Would she call him after the audition? If he didn't hear from her by tonight maybe he'd call her.

He slowly shook his head, rejecting that idea. He'd made the last move with the card and gift. It was up to her now to decide if she wanted something more in their relationship.

"Do you want me to unlock the front door? It's a little past nine." Mandy walked toward him from the back of the store where she had been dusting and straightening the gift section.

"Sure." He passed her the keys. These early holiday hours made it a long day, but at least their sales numbers were increasing.

"Everything okay, boss? You look a little green around the gills."

He rubbed his eyes. "I'm okay." But he hadn't slept much last night and it obviously showed.

Mandy unlocked the front door and flipped the OPEN

sign. The door burst open, setting the bell jingling. Marian, Irene, Barb and Hannah trooped in and headed straight for the sales counter.

Ross sprung from his stool. "Marian, what are you doing here? I thought the doctor said you were supposed to stay home and take it easy."

"He did, but I'm fine. The Treasures chauffeured me."

"We've got a bone to pick with you." Barb sent him a stern glance.

"Me?" Ross blinked and looked around the group.

"George called this morning," Marian said. "He told me about Ray's offer to turn his photo studio over to you." She placed her good hand on her hip. "How could you turn that down?"

Surprise rippled through Ross. He hadn't expected George to tell Marian. "I didn't think it was the right time to leave, especially when you've got your arm in a sling and Adrie is headed out of town."

Barb crossed her arms. "We think you ought to reconsider."

Irene's eyes widened and she sent him a sweet smile. "It's a perfect opportunity for you."

"Remember how much you loved having your own studio at the Arts Center?" Hannah gave him an encouraging nod. "This is your chance for a fresh start."

Ross rubbed his chin. "But I don't see how it would work. Mandy can't run the store on her own, Marian can't carry boxes of books, and Adrie...might be moving to Portland."

"You're right," Marian said. "And that's why these ladies are volunteering to help out until I'm ready to come back to work. I'll hire a new manager. Don't worry about that. If you'll stay through Christmas, we can free you up so you can take over for Ray in January."

Ross slowly shook his head. "Wow, I don't know what to say."

Irene clasped her hands to her chest. "Say yes, and promise you'll call Ray today."

"But I'm not sure his offer still stands. He was talking about closing the studio and selling the building."

Marian tipped her head and smiled. "I happen to have a little influence with George, and I'm sure he can convince Ray to give you some more time."

Ross's throat clogged. He stepped forward and hugged Marian. "Thank you."

"No need to thank me. It's the right thing to do." She smiled up at him and gave him a quick peck on the cheek. "The girls and I haven't had our coffee yet, so we're—"

The bell over the front door jingled again, and they all turned toward the door.

Adrie stepped inside wearing her lavender ski coat with a purple scarf around her neck. The tip of her nose and her cheeks glowed a pretty pink from the cold. "How come the back door's still locked?"

He blinked and his mouth dropped open. "Adrie? What are you doing here?"

She walked toward him, her blue eyes twinkling with starry light and her smile glowing like she had discovered a wonderful secret. "I got as far as Everett, then I stopped for gas and found the envelope and this." She lifted her hand and touched the sea glass beads around her neck. "As soon as I read your note I knew I had the answer to my prayer."

He stepped around the counter and walked toward her. "What prayer? What do you mean?"

They met in the fiction section, and she reached for his hands. "I asked the Lord to stop me if I was headed in the wrong direction. And that's just what He did."

"But what about the audition?"

Tears misted her eyes, and she sent him a tremulous smile. "I'm not going."

"Oh, Adrie, are you sure? I don't want to hold you back from following your dream."

She sniffed and shook her head. "You're not holding me back. You opened the door to your heart and helped me believe in love again. That's the only dream I want."

His heart swelled. He leaned down and kissed her, and she tasted like cinnamon and sugar and all the sweetness his heart could ever hold.

Marian, Irene, Barb and Hannah broke out with clapping and cheers.

Adrie laughed softly and rested her forehead against his. "You know they planned this from the first day we met."

He grinned and winked at her. "They're not the only ones." Then he kissed her once more, just to be sure she knew how glad he was that she'd turned her car around and driven back home to Fairhaven.

Adrie couldn't stop smiling and laughing as she made the rounds to hug Irene, Barb and Hannah. Finally she faced her grandmother with glistening eyes. "Thanks for praying for me, Nana."

"You're welcome, sweetie. That's what grandmas do." She hugged Adrie, then turned to Ross. "Why don't you take the rest of the morning off? Go out for breakfast or take a walk. The girls and I can stay and run the store."

Ross sent Marian a pointed look. "Only if you promise to sit in the café and not do too much."

Barb slipped her arm around Marian's shoulder. "We'll make sure she behaves herself."

"Are you sure you want to stay, Nana? Ross and I could drive you home."

"I'll be fine. I've missed playing Scrabble with the Treasures." Nana shooed them toward the back door. "Go on. I'm sure you two have a lot to talk about."

"Okay." Adrie smiled up at Ross.

He chuckled as he grabbed his coat off the hook by the office. "How about driving down to the bay?"

"That sounds perfect."

Ten minutes later they strolled down Taylor Avenue Dock as a cool breeze blew in from the bay. Adrie tugged her hat down over her ears, thankful they'd both worn warm coats and scarves. They stopped and leaned against the railing, gazing out across the rippling water toward the misty blue San Juan Islands.

"I love coming here." Adrie pulled in a deep breath of fresh, salty air.

Ross moved in closer until his shoulder touched hers. "It's a beautiful spot."

She looked up at him, her heart overflowing. "There's no one I'd rather share it with than you."

Tenderness and affection flowed from his eyes. "I'm sure glad you came back, but I'm still trying to figure out why you changed your mind."

"Maybe I just needed to take that drive and be quiet so God had a chance to speak to me."

Ross grinned. "What did He say?"

"Well, it wasn't an audible voice, but He gave me a strong, clear impression in my heart."

Ross nodded, encouraging her to continue.

"He helped me see my music is a gift from Him. He wants me to enjoy it and use it to bless others. I could do that by playing in the Oregon Symphony, or I could do that right here in Fairhaven. The choice was up to me."

He smiled, his eyes filling with delight. "And you chose Fairhaven."

She nodded. "I love playing at church and being part of the worship team. I don't want to give that up. And I like giving Amber lessons. Maybe I could do that for other foster kids who love music and don't have that opportunity. And if I still have the urge to play more than that, I could put my name out to play at weddings and special events, and even try out for the Whatcom Symphony."

"That sounds great, but it's not exactly what you planned. Are you sure that will be enough for you?"

She tightened her hold on his hand and nodded. "I want to stay here with you and give our relationship a chance. And I want to make sure you can see your dreams fulfilled with your own studio. I'll stay at the store and help train a new manager."

He looked away, and his Adam's apple bobbed in his throat. "Thank you, Adrie. That means more than I can say."

She waited until he looked at her again. "When I read your note, and you said you loved me, that helped me see I could have the future I really wanted. It also helped me realize my significance doesn't come from where I play my music or even *if* I play. God loves me. I am His daughter. Even if I never played another note, He would still love me. I'm His child, and that's enough for me."

"Wow, that's deep."

She looked into his eyes. "Thank you for waiting, and for being my friend and giving me time to figure this out. That means the world to me."

"You are so worth waiting for." He placed his arm around her shoulder and drew her closer. "I about died watching you pull out of the parking lot this morning."

"You were watching?"

"Of course. I had to catch one more glimpse of the girl I love."

Adrie smiled up at him. "Well, she loves you, too." Then she stood on tiptoe and kissed him, and in her heart she knew she had finally found a man worthy of her trust and love.

* * * * *

Dear Reader,

Thanks for taking the journey back to Fairhaven with me! I hope you enjoyed getting to know Adrie, Ross, Marian, George and the rest of the Bayside Treasures. Their story highlights the blessing of friendship and shows how much we need each other to make it through the ups and downs of life. I hope you learned along with Adrie more about the importance of prayer and seeking God for direction in your life, especially when you make plans and face important decisions. God delights in guiding and directing us along the best path for our life. His love is a wonderful anchor that holds us and keeps us close to Him no matter where we go.

Did you read the first story set in Fairhaven featuring Rachel and Cam? If not, I encourage you to pick up a copy of *Seeking His Love*. Be watching for my next book set in Fairhaven in late 2012. Until then, I enjoy hearing from my readers. You may contact me through my website, www.carrieturansky.com.

Until next time, happy reading!
Carrie Turansky

Questions for Discussion

1. When Adrie first meets Ross, he reminds her of her ex-fiancé, and it is a challenge for her to get over that impression and trust Ross. Have you ever distanced yourself from someone because they reminded you of someone else? Did you overcome your discomfort? If so, how?

2. Ross has to close his photography studio because of a downturn in the economy and take on a new job as manager of Bayside Books. Are you working at the job that you first trained for, or have you switched careers like Ross? How has that worked for you?

3. Marian believes Bayside Books is not just a business, it is a ministry, and she wanted to hire a manager who could care for people and encourage them spiritually. Do you consider your job a ministry? What are some ways you could help and encourage people where you work?

4. Adrie thinks Ross won't be a good manager because he is a young Christian and he isn't familiar with Christian publishing. Is that true? What skills and talents does Ross have that help him as a manager?

5. Cam's friendship with Ross plays an important role in the story. How does Cam help Ross?

6. Ross struggles in his relationship with his father. What do you believe were the main issues they needed to work out so they could grow closer?

7. Adrie worked toward her goal of playing her flute professionally for many years. But as the story progresses, she begins to wonder if that was the right path for her life. What caused her to question her goal?

8. Adrie spent many years in Kenya when she was growing up. How did this impact her? Have you ever visited another country? How did it impact you?

9. Adrie is initially upset when her grandmother starts seeing George Bradford. Why do you think that bothers her? Are her reasons valid?

10. Ross uses his skills as a photographer to help foster children, even though he isn't paid. What are some skills that you might be able to use to help others?

11. Adrie and Ross both pray and ask God to guide them as they make decisions about their future. When was the last time you asked God to help you make a decision or give you direction? How did that turn out for you?

12. As the story ends, Adrie realizes her significance doesn't come from playing with a symphony; it comes from her relationship with God and His love for her. How does your relationship with God meet some of your needs for significance? What's one thing you could do to grow closer to God?

INSPIRATIONAL

Love Inspired®

celebrating 15 YEARS

COMING NEXT MONTH
AVAILABLE MARCH 27, 2012

HER LONE STAR COWBOY
Mule Hollow Homecoming
Debra Clopton

A LOVE REKINDLED
A Town Called Hope
Margaret Daley

SWEETHEART REUNION
Lenora Worth

REDEMPTION RANCH
Leann Harris

HER FAMILY WISH
Betsy St. Amant

LOVE OF A LIFETIME
Carol Voss

LICNM0312

REQUEST YOUR FREE BOOKS!

2 FREE INSPIRATIONAL NOVELS
PLUS 2
FREE
MYSTERY GIFTS

Love Inspired.

YES! Please send me 2 FREE Love Inspired® novels and my 2 FREE mystery gifts (gifts are worth about $10). After receiving them, if I don't wish to receive any more books, I can return the shipping statement marked "cancel." If I don't cancel, I will receive 6 brand-new novels every month and be billed just $4.49 per book in the U.S. or $4.99 per book in Canada. That's a saving of at least 22% off the cover price. It's quite a bargain! Shipping and handling is just 50¢ per book in the U.S. and 75¢ per book in Canada.* I understand that accepting the 2 free books and gifts places me under no obligation to buy anything. I can always return a shipment and cancel at any time. Even if I never buy another book, the two free books and gifts are mine to keep forever.

105/305 IDN FEGR

Name	(PLEASE PRINT)	
Address		Apt. #
City	State/Prov.	Zip/Postal Code

Signature (if under 18, a parent or guardian must sign)

Mail to the **Reader Service:**
IN U.S.A.: P.O. Box 1867, Buffalo, NY 14240-1867
IN CANADA: P.O. Box 609, Fort Erie, Ontario L2A 5X3

Not valid for current subscribers to Love Inspired books.

**Are you a subscriber to Love Inspired books
and want to receive the larger-print edition?
Call 1-800-873-8635 or visit www.ReaderService.com.**

* Terms and prices subject to change without notice. Prices do not include applicable taxes. Sales tax applicable in N.Y. Canadian residents will be charged applicable taxes. Offer not valid in Quebec. This offer is limited to one order per household. All orders subject to credit approval. Credit or debit balances in a customer's account(s) may be offset by any other outstanding balance owed by or to the customer. Please allow 4 to 6 weeks for delivery. Offer available while quantities last.

Your Privacy—The Reader Service is committed to protecting your privacy. Our Privacy Policy is available online at www.ReaderService.com or upon request from the Reader Service.

We make a portion of our mailing list available to reputable third parties that offer products we believe may interest you. If you prefer that we not exchange your name with third parties, or if you wish to clarify or modify your communication preferences, please visit us at www.ReaderService.com/consumerschoice or write to us at Reader Service Preference Service, P.O. Box 9062, Buffalo, NY 14269. Include your complete name and address.

LIREG11B

Kim Walters needs Zane Davidson's help. After a devastating hurricane, Kim's family is struggling to rebuild their home, and Zane is a successful contractor. But it's been fifteen years since they were high school sweethearts and their past problems aren't about to magically melt away. Can Kim and Zane find the faith to believe that some things work better the second time around?

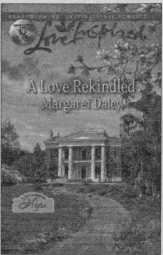

A Love Rekindled
by Margaret Daley